JUDGES

Also in English Translation

Andrea Camilleri
Carlo Lucarelli
Giancarlo De Cataldo

JUDGES

Translated from the Italian by Joseph Farrell,
Alan Thawley and Eileen Horne

MacLehose Press
New York • London

MacLehose Press
An imprint of Quercus
New York • London

Copyright © 2011 Giulio Einaudi editore s.p.a., Torino
First published in the United States by Quercus in 2015

First published in the Italian language as *Giudici* by Giulio Einaudi editore s.p.a., Torino in 2011

Judge Surra
Copyright © 2011 Andrea Camilleri
English translation copyright © 2014 by Joseph Farrell
The Bambina
Copyright © 2011 Carlo Lucarelli
Published by arrangement with Roberto Santachiara Agenzia Letteraria, Pavia
English translation copyright © 2014 by Alan Thawley
The Triple Dream of the Prosecutor
Copyright © 2011 Giancarlo De Cataldo
English translation copyright © 2014 by Eileen Horne

ISBN 978-1-62365-629-4

Library of Congress Control Number: 2015946255

Distributed in the United States and Canada by
Hachette Book Group
1290 Avenue of the Americas
New York, NY 10104

Manufactured in the United States

10 9 8 7 6 5 4 3 2 1

www.quercus.com

CONTENTS

TRANSLATOR'S NOTE

As you read this collection, you will come across familiar figures like judges, magistrates and prosecutors, but the English and Italian terms do not necessarily correspond.

Whilst a long discussion of the differences between our legal systems would be off-putting and unnecessary, a little background information might be helpful. In Italy, *giudici* (judges) and *procuratori* (public prosecutors) are colleagues: both roles come under the independent institution known as the *magistratura*, and in fact prosecutors are often referred to as judges in everyday usage.

Under the Napoleonic Code, which formed the basis for the Italian system, judges performed an investigative role as well as presiding over trials and handing down sentences. The protagonist of the second story is a *giudice istruttore*, usually rendered in English as "examining magistrate," whose job is to conduct an impartial investigation into the facts of a case, although the role was actually abolished in the late 1980s.

Another feature of the Italian system touched upon in the stories is the co-existence of two separate national police forces: the *carabinieri* are a military police force, whereas the *polizia di stato* (state police) are now a civilian force. Both have a long history, and have developed sometimes overlapping responsibilities, which can lead to rivalry and confusion.

Alan Thawley

Andrea Camilleri

JUDGE SURRA

1

Judge Surra arrived in Montelusa from Turin a fortnight after the first prefect of the United Italy, a Florentine called Falconcini, had taken up his post on the island.

Even before the judge reached the town, a few things about him became known. How? By what means? Perhaps one of the staff who came with Falconcini had known him previously and spread the word.

For instance, it became known that even though his Christian and family names were Sardinian, he himself was not—his great-grandfather on his father's side, who was from Iglesias, and who had moved to Turin when the Piedmontese bartered Sicily for Sardinia, had children with a Turinese woman and never again ventured away from the city.

It was also established that Judge Surra was around fifty, that he was a little less than average height, that he invariably dressed soberly, that he was married with one son who was a lawyer but that he would be coming to Montelusa on his own.

At least to begin with.

Further, that he was a man of few words and kept himself to himself.

On the other hand, little was known about him as a judge, since he had always been employed inside the ministry and had not seen service in a courtroom.

The challenge facing him on his arrival was anything but straightforward. It consisted in totally reconstructing a court of law which quite simply no longer existed. In plain terms, the task was to replace the previous president of the court, Fallarino, whom Garibaldi's followers wished to arrest on account of his intractably pro-Bourbon views—he had refused to recognise the Savoy monarchy and had in consequence resigned; then to bring back those judges who had worked with the Bourbons and who would be happy to continue in post in the new state, but only after their outlook had been changed; and finally to introduce the Piedmontese code of law, which was still unknown to judges and lawyers alike.

Obviously, even in the nobles' club, whose membership consisted not only of noblemen but also of wealthy landowners and tradesmen, there was much discussion about the judge who was due to arrive. "Surra," Don Agatino Smecca said. "In our towns and villages that's a word meaning 'belly' which, as you all know, is the most delicate and tasty part of the tuna fish. So, going by his surname, this judge is very promising."

"You are talking like that because you're a man of the sea," Don Clemente Sommartino said. "But I'm a man of the fields, a peasant, and I'm here to tell you that 'surra' is the name of a bitter, smelly herb which, when chickens eat it, gives their eggs a nasty taste that makes you spit them out. So his surname, as far as I'm concerned, promises nothing good at all."

"That's enough of this nonsense. A name tells you nothing about the person who bears it," Bonocore, the sulphur dealer, cut in. "You remember that judge who was called Benevolo but who was anything but? He never acquitted anyone, and was worse than an executioner."

"That's true enough," Don Clemente thought to himself. "And while we're at it, you're called Bonocore, and far from having a good heart as your name implies, you bankrupted two of your colleagues."

But he did not say a word.

When the ship from Palermo docked at Vigàta, a clerk from the prefect's office introduced himself to the judge.

"His Excellency Falconcini has procured comfortable lodgings for you in Montelusa. I'd be delighted to take you there in my carriage. You get in; I'll load up your luggage."

The apartment in the upper city, in the vicinity of the cathedral, turned out to be comfortable, spacious and elegantly appointed with eighteenth-century furniture. It was part of the palace belonging to the Marchese Bontadini, but it was completely self-contained, with its own door along from the main entrance.

Before leaving him, the clerk handed him a card from the prefect. It informed him that in the stables on the far side of the street, opposite the entrance to the house, a carriage, a mule and coachman by the name of Attanasio, a trustworthy person, had been put at his disposal.

The judge changed his clothes and crossed to the stables.

"At your service. I am Attanasio. Do you require the carriage?" Asking the questions was a curly-haired man of some forty years of age with intelligent eyes, dressed in livery.

"No, I'd rather go on foot. But would you mind doing me two favours?"

"You have only to ask, your Excellency."

"I require the services of a woman to clean the apartment and keep it tidy. And to prepare my meals, because I don't like eating out."

"Excellency, I will tell my wife, Pippina."

"If she could come tomorrow morning at seven-thirty . . ."

"Very well."

"And then I would like to purchase a pointer dog, but you would need to look after it for me somewhere else."

"I will have three or four dogs brought along no later than tomorrow, and you can make your choice. And I will be happy to look after it."

The judge thanked him and was about to go when Attanasio gave himself a slap on the forehead.

"Ah, Excellency, I forgot. Earlier today, a servant from the Bontadini Palace gave me this, and said to tell you he found it under the main door."

He pulled out a letter and handed it to him.

Surra looked at him in amazement. How could this be? They knew his address even before he had arrived.

The letter had been delivered by hand. The address was printed and read: To His Excellency Efisio Surra, Palazzo Bontadini, The City.

The judge was certain the letter would be anonymous. Indeed it was.

Excellency, what happened to the papers relating to the hearings in the cases of Milioto, Savastano, Curreli and Costantino? Why not discuss it with Don Emanuele Lonero, known as Don Nené?

A friend of Justice.

He slipped it into his pocket and went off to meet the prefect.

Who did not have good news for him.

Of all the court's staff, only the head clerk, three assistant clerks, two ushers, four court officers, two presiding judges and four judges were prepared to cooperate with the new government.

In principle, the court was capable of being reactivated, but in practice it was not at all easy to see how this would work. The prefect assigned to the court a corps of one maresciallo and four carabinieri. It was the best he could do. Judge Surra asked for the address of the previous president of the court, Fallarino, and then told maresciallo Solano, who had in the meantime been introduced to him, to instruct those who were willing to work with him to present themselves at the court the following morning at nine o'clock.

Since the invitation from the prefect was for dinner, he was left with some time on his hands. He wrote to the ex-president of the court, Saverio Fallarino, requesting the pleasure of a meeting, and told one of the carabinieri to deliver it.

The reply was brought by the same man: President Fallarino would meet him at his house at five o'clock the following day.

When the judge left the prefecture, it was after nine o'clock.

It was such a lovely night that he felt inclined to go for a stroll along the *corso*. He was surprised to find so many people about, weaving in and out in a continual ballet of deft moves, bows, smiles and compliments.

The thing which most powerfully attracted his attention was the window of a big caffè with its display of multi-coloured cakes. The judge had one vice, a badly kept secret: an overwhelming fondness for sweet things. It had been the cause of many quarrels with his wife, who feared for his health. He saw before him a pile of strange sweets—brownish tubes of crisp pastry of

about twenty centimetres in length, filled with white cream and
flecked on the sides with tiny pieces of candied fruit.

He could not resist and went in. The tables were all taken.
When they set eyes on him, the company fell silent for a moment,
but then the conversation struck up again.

"What are those cakes called?" he said to a waiter behind the
counter.

"*Cannoli*, Excellency."

Could they possibly have recognised him already?

"I'll have one."

He ate it standing at the bar. Madonna! It was really good.

"I'll have another."

He went over to the till to pay, but the cashier waved him
away. "It's been paid for."

"Paid for? By whom?" The judge could not conceal his
disbelief.

"By Don Nené Lonero."

The judge turned and looked around the room. At one table
four men were seated, one with a beret and two with hats. A
stocky fifty-year-old man, with fair skin and reddish hair, rose
to his feet, removed his hat and said: "Accept it as a gesture of
welcome."

Without replying, the judge turned back to the cashier and
stared him straight in the face. The cashier felt a cold quiver run
down his spine. What eyes that man had! Blue and ice-cold, like
the sky on a winter's morning. Then, without another word,
Surra placed a large coin in front of him. The cashier, head
bowed, gave him his change. The judge moved slowly over to
the table where Don Nené was still on his feet, glowering at the
snub. Inside the caffè, there fell a silence that could have been
cut with a knife.

"Are you Emanuele Lonero?"

"I am."

"I'd like to take advantage of this opportunity," the judge said, with a courteous smile.

"To do what?" Don Nené asked.

"Be patient one moment."

He took the anonymous letter from his pocket, opened it out, took his glasses from his waistcoat pocket, calmly put them on and finally spoke in a voice loud enough for everyone to hear: "I do not know who each of you is, and I have no wish to know, but it appears that you have unlawfully taken the records of the hearings of proceedings against Milioto, Savastano, Curreli and Costantino. Be good enough to return them to the court within the next twenty-four hours."

He replaced the letter in his pocket, took off his glasses, returned them to his waistcoat, turned his back on Don Nené, who stood rooted to the spot, and went out.

He understood immediately that he had committed a bad mistake.

He should have taken only one *cannolo*, not two. If he went to lie down straightaway, with his stomach bloated by the ricotta, he would never get to sleep. There was nothing for it but to walk about for at least an hour.

The third time he came back up the *corso*, two well-dressed men coming towards him changed direction slightly so that one of them almost brushed against him.

It was at that point that the judge heard a voice say almost in a whisper, "Bravo! You deserve respect."

He stopped in his tracks, astounded. Had someone really said to him—Bravo! Why? What had he done? He could find no explanation. Perhaps eating two *cannoli* one after the other was a proof of virility in these parts? It would be no easy feat to understand them, these Sicilians.

2

HE WAS AWAKENED AT SIX BY AN EAR-SPLITTING YELL FROM the street below. He jumped out of bed, threw open the window and looked down. The shout came from a peasant holding under his arm a basket filled with eggs. The yell rang out once more. In the house opposite, a woman leant over a balcony ringed with flowers and lowered down a basket attached to a length of rope. The peasant picked out the cash inside, replaced it with four eggs and continued on his way. The judge was about to close the window again when a doleful female howl sounded along the street. He turned back to see an aged woman dressed in rags selling vegetables. What made them wail in that way when advertising their wares?

He noticed that along the street they were erecting stalls for the market. He went back to bed for a little before getting up to wash and dress. At seven-thirty, he heard a knock at the door. He went over to open it.

"At your service. My name's Pippina."

She was stout, smiling and pleasant, and inspired trust. The judge asked how much she would expect on a monthly basis for her work, and received in reply an incredibly low figure. The judge told her what he preferred to eat at lunch and dinner and gave her money for the purchases. He also gave her the house keys, he himself already having another set. When the woman left, he wrote a letter to his wife, and at quarter to nine got ready to go out. He opened the door and found Attanasio standing there.

"I was just coming, Excellency."

"I haven't any time for the dog now."

"I'm not here about the dog," Attanasio replied, brusquely.

"What, then?"

"This morning, it'd be better for Your Excellency to take the carriage to the court."

"Why? It's not raining. It's a lovely day."

"Trust me. Take the carriage."

The judge grew irritated. What absurd airs this Attanasio was giving himself!

"That's enough. I've decided to go on foot."

"Then will Your Excellency allow me to accompany you?"

"No," he replied firmly.

Attanasio stretched out his arms in resignation, and let him pass.

The street was now very busy. There were not only women but also many men circulating among the stalls. At one, there were some highly coloured cakes on sale. He hesitated a moment, then gave a deep sigh.

The street was on a slight incline, and the stalls ended at a curve in the road. Three men were standing there chatting among themselves, with another five further on who seemed to have nothing to do, but who appeared to be waiting for somebody or something. One of the three came forward with a bow.

"Good morning, Judge Surra."

Who could he be? Surra returned the greeting, raising his hat for a moment then replacing it.

Just as he took away his hand, the hat was blown away violently, as though caught by a sudden gust of wind.

At the same time, he heard a dry crack, like a branch snapping, coming from somewhere high above him, to one side.

He thought he saw a vase of flowers falling from a balcony towards his head.

He leapt to one side, went over to pick up his hat and replaced it on his head.

Now there was no-one on the street.

All vanished in a trice. How could that be? How odd!

Nicolosi, the head clerk, was standing at the door of the court to receive him. He introduced him to the three assistant clerks and the two ushers. Lined up one alongside the other, the six immediately broke into applause. Taken aback, the judge could do no more than mutter a word of thanks.

"Your hat, Excellency," Nicolosi said respectfully.

The judge, even more astounded, took it off and gave it to him. What strange habits they had in these parts! What curious rituals!

"We should place it in a glass display case, like a relic," Nicolosi went on.

Were they mad? Or was this a joke in dubious taste? Or was it part of some ceremony of welcome?

"But I need my hat," the judge protested.

"You need a new one, because this one . . . Don't you see, Excellency?"

And he showed it to him. Only then did the judge notice that a piece was missing from the back rim. Clearly, when it had blown off, it had ended up against some sharp edge. A pity, for he had had it no more than three months.

"Is everyone else here?"

"Every one of them, Excellency. They're waiting for you in the meeting room."

"The carabinieri?"

"They're here too. They're clearing out three rooms on the far side of the yard for use as their offices."

"Good. Take me to meet them, will you?"

The meeting was fairly short, no more than an hour. More than anything else, it was an opportunity for each side to get to know the other. Just as they were winding up, two men came in to receive an enthusiastic greeting from those present. Paolantonio, presiding judge in the local divisional court, introduced them to Surra. The newcomers were two further judges, Moresco and Colla, who had decided to cooperate.

"After all that's been going on, we felt we really ought to be here," Colla said, shaking his hand.

What had been going on? Surra was bewildered, but he preferred to remain silent.

The meeting broke up, but there was a general willingness to press on with unfinished work. They agreed to meet again at the same time the following day.

Judge Surra had asked Nicolosi to draw up an inventory of all that was required to get the court in working order. He would make a withdrawal from the budget set aside in the prefecture.

Nicolosi handed it to him and the judge then asked if he could visit the court building itself.

The disorder was indescribable. Cabinets thrown open with registers and folders hanging out, case notes and files spilling out from them onto the floor . . . dossiers everywhere, in the corridors, on the windowsills, in the packed cupboards . . . complete chaos.

Even on the most optimistic assessment, it would take the minimum of a week to make any headway.

"Get the ushers and carabinieri as well as the clerks to give you a hand. If need be, call in some men to do the heavy lifting work. And hire some women to clean up."

He had scarcely left himself enough time to buy a new hat before returning home for lunch.

Which was simple but delicious. That Pippina knew her business—the apartment had been thoroughly tidied too. He took a little rest, then wrote minutes of the morning meeting. He freshened himself up before going over to the stables.

"Attanasio, do you know where President Fallarino lives?"

"Yes, Excellency. He has a villa outside the town."

"Let's go there."

"To what do I owe this honour?"

Ex-President Fallarino was a tall, fair, thin, severe and imposing man. He received Surra in a book-lined study.

"In the first place, I regarded it as a duty to come and pay my respects."

"And in the second place?"

If he imagined he would cause Surra to lose his composure by his abrupt manners, he was mistaken. "To ask if you would have the courtesy to assist me."

"Me, assist you? But you must know who I am . . ."

"Your Honour," the judge interrupted him firmly, "I am aware of your political convictions and, although my ideas are opposed to yours, I admire the consistency of your conduct. But we do have one thing in common."

"That is?"

"A sincere, respectful love of justice."

"I will not return to the court," Fallarino replied after a brief pause.

"I do not ask that of you. But justice is done by men, and I do not know the men who have chosen to resume service with me."

"In the meeting this morning, did you tell them you'd be coming to see me?"

So he knew about the meeting!

"I did not consider it advisable."

"That was wise."

"Why?"

"Not all of them would have approved. You know better than me that a court of law works best when there is mutual respect and esteem among the men at every level. Here, especially recently, that esteem has been in short supply, and incomers have been put in charge."

"It's the same everywhere."

"Yes, but more so here than elsewhere. At any rate, you will appreciate that I cannot assist you. Some of those who were there this morning were my most ferocious accusers. Any judgement on them coming from me would be liable to be viewed as partisan. I am grateful for your trust, but my reply is—I can be of no assistance."

"Give me at least one name. Among those who attended today's meeting, who would be most opposed to my coming here?"

Fallarino's face softened momentarily into the faintest of smiles.

"You are very shrewd. Paolantonio."

"May I ask one more favour and then I'll leave you in peace. Read this."

He pulled the anonymous letter from his pocket and handed it to Fallarino, who read it and gave it back.

"What do you think?" Surra asked.

"It's puzzling."

"Why?"

"Because the anonymous writer does not explain exactly how things went. It was this that led you astray last night in the Caffè *Arnone* when you asked Don Nené to return the papers which had been unlawfully removed."

The judge was taken aback. So he knew this too!

"And how did things go exactly?"

"Don Nené Lonero courteously requested these papers from one of our judges, who with equal courtesy acceded to the request."

"But this is a very serious crime!" Surra said. "Why did those papers interest him?"

"Presumably because they related to trials for murder or kidnap, very serious crimes indeed. I had instituted the enquiries myself. Against members of the brotherhood of which Don Nené is head."

"And what is this brotherhood?" the judge asked.

"You are plainly unaware of the report drawn up by Don Pietro Ulloa, the procurator general at Trapani. It is highly instructive, and the situation has not changed in any way since then."

He got to his feet, walked over to his bookcase and came back with a book in his hand.

"Let me make you a present of it. I have another copy."

He remained standing, indicating that the visit was over. Surra too got up.

"You cannot refuse to give me the name of the person who gave the papers to Lonero. That would constitute conspiracy."

"I have already given you one name. That will suffice." Fallarino smiled again and offered him his hand.

3

However, he insisted on accompanying him to the carriage.

"Come and see me any time you wish," he said, once again shaking his hand.

"Thank you. I will take advantage of that invitation."

Just as the carriage was beginning to move off, Fallarino stepped onto the footboard, leant forward and looking Surra in the face said quietly: "I wish I'd had your courage."

And he got down.

The judge was shaken by that expression. Clearly, to bring the court to a point where it could operate normally would require clarity of thought, perseverance, determination, patience . . . but courage? That was overdoing it! What a weighty word! Yes, Sicilians tended to exaggerate, to dramatise, as he was beginning to understand.

"Where now?" Attanasio asked.

"To the prefecture."

★ ★ ★

It took less than a quarter of an hour for the news of the shots
fired at Judge Surra to spread all over the town.

The only one who was unaware of it was Surra himself, but
it did not occur to a single soul that he had not understood that
he had been the object of an attempt on his life, and in consequence his behaviour enlivened the discussion that afternoon at
the Nobles' Club.

"It's exactly the same as a game of chess," Don Agatino Smecca
said. "One of the players is none other than our judge Surra who,
at the Caffè *Arnone,* issued a public challenge to Don Nené
Lonero. It was the judge who made the first move by asking for
the return of the papers. A bold challenge, there's no denying
it. And one which the recipient accepted, and this morning he
made his move by having Surra shot at."

"That's right," Don Clemente Sommartino replied. "But
you've got to add that the second move should be described
as interlocutory. It was a warning, because it's obvious to the
whole world that if Don Nené wanted him killed, he was a
dead man." "Right enough," Professor Sciacca said, "but this
time I don't think Don Nené is going to find it so easy to win
this particular game. I would even go so far as to say there's
no way of knowing who's going to come out on top. Judge
Surra might look as though he's nothing, but he must have
balls of iron."

"Iron! Reinforced steel!" Don Arturo Siccia cut in. "Listen
to me. Did you hear what the eye witnesses recounted? After
the shots were fired, as fresh and cool as a quartered chicken on
a block, he bent down, picked up his hat, stuck it on his head
without deigning even to glance at it, and went on his way to
the court without uttering a word. What does he have in his
veins? Ice?"

"If you want to know, I was there during the scene the other evening in the Caffè *Arnone*," Doctor Piscopo said. "Mother of God, you should have seen him, icy-cold he was as he ordered Don Nené to hand back the papers. He even had a smile on his lips as he spoke."

"That's a man who's not afraid of a living soul! And he's going to give Don Nené just enough rope to hang himself," Don Agatino Smecca said.

They all nodded.

The prefect was not at home. He was out of town and due back late. The judge took the money for the repairs to the courtroom to hand over to Nicolosi, but before returning home, he stopped at the Caffè *Arnone* to get them to wrap up two *cannoli* for him. So what if they would lie heavily on his stomach?

As he made his way home, he could not fail to notice a certain change in the attitude of passers-by towards him. Some, a clear majority, greeted him with evident warmth and even gave him a friendly smile, while a minority ostentatiously ignored him, turning away or hurriedly crossing the street to avoid him.

He could not understand what was going on.

God Almighty, was he not the same Surra he had been the night before? What was different about him? He had done nothing to justify such clear evidence of hostility from some and of friendliness from others.

A friend in Turin, himself a Sicilian, had warned him that Sicilians are much more volatile than they wish to appear. But how far did this go? Was there something amiss in his own behaviour? Perhaps some people were upset at his excessive fondness for *cannoli*, while others were pleased at his appreciation of a local product?

Ah well! He would never manage to fathom them!

He dined at home and intended to start reading the book which Fallarino had given him.

But he changed his mind and set to thinking how he should conduct himself with regard to Presiding Judge Paolantonio.

Two hours later, he believed he had come up with a solution and went to sleep.

"I am sorry to have to tell you that your request to be readmitted to judicial service has been rejected."

Paolantonio turned pale.

"May I ask why?"

"You are fully entitled to know. You took possession, unlawfully, of court papers relating to a case which was still *sub judice* and thus covered by requirements of confidentiality, and you handed them to a third party when requested. I have no doubt you were perfectly aware of the gravity of the crime you were committing."

The judge found it hard to reply. He wiped his sweating forehead with a handkerchief.

"There are some matters which . . . even against your own will . . ."

"There can be no justification for what you have done," Surra cut him short. "I would also advise you that I consider it my duty to institute proceedings against you for this offence."

Paolantonio's face turned ashen.

"I . . . I beg you to spare me this . . ."

Judge Surra stared at him. Paolantonio trembled and fell silent.

"There might be a solution."

"Tell me and I'll . . ."

"Have the papers returned and bring them to me. Within the next two hours. You can take two of the clerks with you."

He left the man struggling to rise from his seat, and went into the meeting room where they were all waiting for him.

"I apologise for being late, but I have just had a conversation with Judge Paolantonio. I informed him that his request for readmission to judicial duties has been refused. I believe you all know, or at least can guess, the reasons. Now, to work."

As the meeting was breaking up, Nicolosi approached to whisper something in his ear. They agreed to meet again the following morning. For the moment it was better to leave the offices free to allow the cleaning ladies to get on with their work.

"Would Judges Moresco, Colla, Di Betta and Consolato be kind enough to come with me?"

They followed him out.

The four files which had gone missing were there on Judge Surra's desk. They seemed to be in perfect order.

"Gentlemen, these are the case reports which were illicitly removed and which I have had brought back."

The four judges glanced at each other stunned and amazed. What manner of man was this?

"Did you call in the carabinieri?" Colla asked.

"There was no need."

He had managed to intimidate a man like Don Nené, on his own, without the backing of the police!

"I would like each of you, as soon as we are able to operate properly, to take responsibility for one of these four cases. I would like you to give them absolute priority. For the moment, I consider it prudent to keep these folders here, in my office, in the green cabinet, the only one for which I have a key. Good day, gentlemen."

When the judges left the room, he called two clerks, asked them to clear one shelf of the green cabinet behind his desk, and had them place the four folders there. He locked it and put the key in his pocket.

The clerks went out. Surra stayed on a little to check the parcel with the stamps which had just arrived from Turin.

As he got up, the high back of his chair knocked against the doors of the green cabinet.

He moved the chair and the doors swung open.

How was this possible? He had locked it himself!

He attempted to lock it again and only then did he realise that the key turned round and round without engaging. He could not leave the files here, where anyone could get at them. They must be of great importance if the president of a divisional court had been prepared to risk prison to get hold of them.

He went into the corridor. The court offices were empty. Everyone was out at lunch. He noticed that a few metres from his door there was a massive black cupboard. He tried to open it. It was locked, and who knows where the key had ended up?

He had a moment of inspiration.

He went back to his office, took out the key of the green cabinet, put it into the keyhole of the black cupboard and turned it.

The cupboard opened. It was completely empty.

He tried the key again. It worked perfectly.

He moved the files into the black cupboard in the corridor and locked it. In his own office, by stuffing pieces of folded paper at the bottom of the doors, he managed to get them to close.

Then he went off home.

As the judge, savouring every mouthful, tasted for the first time Pippina's fresh ricotta dessert, the news of the dismissal of Judge Paolantonio and of the return of the files went round the town.

Everyone considered Judge Surra's moves to be ingenious and agreed that he had shown himself to be a skilled, astute and cool-headed gambler.

Perhaps the only man capable of making Don Nené lose his head.

"Don't get a rush of blood, and above all don't do anything rash," were the very words spoken by Senator Pasquale Midulla to Don Nené, who stood trembling before him.

"But I can't allow this bastard to spit in my face in front of everybody! I've got to do something. Don't you understand? Otherwise I'll lose face."

He was almost foaming at the mouth.

"Let's go about it this way," the senator said. "Give him a second warning. And if he continues not to understand, I'll have a word with him myself."

4

Judge Surra opened the meeting by announcing two items of news.

The first was that head clerk Nicolosi had managed to locate the register of the trials underway at the time of the interruption of the court's activities, and that consequently the present session would be devoted to an examination of the register, without prejudice to the commitment already made to prioritise the four cases where the files had been removed but then returned.

The second piece of news was that two other magistrates, Di Cagno and Martorana, had applied to be re-admitted to the justiciary, and they would be in attendance at the following day's meeting.

He omitted to say that Di Cagno and Martorana had turned up at his house with a letter from ex-President Fallarino in which he sang their praises. Halfway through the meeting, Nicolosi came in holding a large parcel in both hands.

"A few moments ago, a man delivered this for you. He told me to give it to you personally. He said it's a gift."

"I do not accept gifts. Send it back immediately," Surra said brusquely.

"How can I? There's no indication of the sender and I don't know the man who ..."

"Then throw it out."

"Just a minute," Butera said, presiding judge in another division. "Would it not be a good idea to see what it is before throwing it out?"

"Do you think so?" Surra said, plainly baffled.

"Well, here there are certain customs which ..."

The truth was that each one of them, with the exception of Judge Surra, wanted to see the parcel opened in their presence—they all had a half suspicion of what it was likely to contain.

"Alright then. Open it."

The head clerk placed the parcel in the centre of the table, taking off the wrapping paper to reveal a metal box.

Nicolosi stopped, unsure of what to do next. He too had the same suspicion as the others.

"Well? Open it up," Surra said.

Nicolosi removed the lid of the box.

They all rose to their feet to see, saw and fell back heavily on their chairs, distraught, ashen and silent.

Partially wrapped in pieces of cloth, which had once been white but were now soaked red with blood, lay a neatly severed lamb's head. Its great, staring eyes appeared almost human.

The first to speak was Judge Surra.

"Ah! A lamb's head!" He smiled.

He held his smile as the others remained motionless, frozen by sheer horror and by the appalling significance of the threat.

Judge Surra continued to smile at a now distant memory of home. In his childhood, his grandfather had occasionally persuaded his grandmother to cook a lamb's head, and he would pass some bits to the boy seated beside him. My God, how good they had been! After his grandfather's death, lamb's head had disappeared from the family menu.

"Would any of you like it?" he asked.

They all shook their heads, dismayed, incapable of speech.

"Filipazzo, one of my relatives, eats these things," Nicolosi said at last.

"Good. Give it to him, with my compliments! Right then, gentlemen, shall we resume?"

"In all sincerity, that man scares me. There's something about him which is not quite human," Judge Moresco said to his colleague, Consolato, as they were returning home. Being near neighbours, they were in the habit of walking a bit of the way together.

"He has the same effect on me. He really unnerves me. He could put the fear of God into anybody. He could even smile when faced with a death threat. We were all scared out of our wits, but he just sat there as though he'd been offered a little present which, unhappily, he thought he really ought to decline. Good God, what an attitude! What inhuman courage!

"What can I say? Judge Surra is one of those men who could be called a hero."

"I quite agree with you," Consolato said.

What was Pippina up to? Varying the menu every day to make him sample the full range of Sicilian cuisine? Her *pasta con le sarde* had him licking his lips and drove out all thought of lamb's head. Lunches, dinners, *cannoli* . . . at this rate he would put on a lot of weight before returning to Piedmont.

After lunch, a messenger brought him a card from the prefect, requesting his attendance at the prefecture at three o'clock. Senator Pasquale Midulla, who represented the Montelusa constituency and was also undersecretary at the Ministry of Justice, was about to leave for Rome after a brief visit to his constituents and wished to be briefed on conditions at the court.

"I have put this room at your disposal so that the two of you can talk without being disturbed," the prefect said.

And he left them alone.

Judge Surra, feeling it his duty not to wait for the senator to ask specific questions, gave him a detailed report on the restructuring work, concluding that no later than one week from that day the court would be in a position to resume its activities, albeit only partially.

"And that's where the most awkward problem lies," the senator said.

"Why's that?" the judge said, unsure of himself.

"I mean for you."

"For me? By then we will have resolved the most awkward problems. It's a matter of beginning the normal . . ."

"Normal? Listen, Your Honour, I would like you to reflect on the fact that Sicily is not Piedmont."

"I know," Surra said, his pride stung.

"Let me explain myself better. With us, things are not always as they appear. With you, it's different. With you, white is white and black is black. With us, grey predominates."

"How strange! I thought it was the opposite. Since the day I arrived, there's never been a day of rain. There's been a sun which casts clearly defined shadows."

The senator looked at him bewildered. Had he really not understood or was he only pretending? Yet the judge had a look of such transparency that . . .

"Let me make another attempt to make myself clear. When Ippolito Nievo landed with Garibaldi and saw our young men fighting, he defined them initially as ferocious savages. Later, he changed his mind when he realised that what he was seeing was extreme courage, where death could represent the most longed-for prize. What I mean to say is that there are certain types of behaviour which might appear downright criminal in the eyes of non-Sicilians, but which are often dictated by a deep sense of honour and by a notion of justice which regrettably does not always conform to the code of law."

"If it does not conform to the code, I find it hard to see how it can be called justice," Surra replied simply.

"What was I telling you? We're talking about behaviour which is hard to explain and even downright incomprehensible to those who do not have our mentality. Let me give you another example. Recent years have been, for us, years of the absence of everything, of rules, of laws, in a word, of the State. We would have descended into the most complete disorder if some men of good will had not rolled up their sleeves and taken on themselves the burden of dictating rules and ensuring they were observed. But since these rules were not laid down in the various codes, such men found themselves automatically outside the boundaries of law. And yet they had the merit of . . ."

"Forgive me if I ask a question, Excellency. Would you number Signor Emanuele Lonero among these men of good will?" The senator smiled. This man from Piedmont was not such a fool as he might appear.

"Yes, he is one such. Why not?"

"Because this gentleman procured from a dishonest magistrate some court papers which . . ."

"And that's what I wanted you to see," the senator interjected without a moment's hesitation. "As soon as you asked him, Lonero returned them to you intact. If he took possession of the papers, it was to keep them safe, since the court was no longer guarded. You see how easy it is to fall into misunderstandings?"

"These four cases are clearly close to the heart of Signor Lonero."

"Indeed, because they concern four of his friends and assistants who contributed to the maintenance of law and order, and who worked to ensure harmonious relations between people. For exactly that reason he would like—how can I put this—to see them well treated. I don't say treated with any special partiality, heaven forbid, but treated with due regard for all that they have done . . ."

"Signor Lonero will be pleased to know I have given instructions that those four cases are to be given absolute priority. They will be the first four trials held in the new court at Montelusa. This I can guarantee."

He made a slight bow to the senator, who looked at him dumbfounded, and made his exit.

"Don Nené is too uncouth for a man like Judge Surra," Don Agatino said, growing more excited as he spoke. "Of course he allowed himself a slight smile when he saw the lamb's head! It was the smile of a superior man, that's what it was—the smile of a man who knows he could leave his opponent twisting in the wind as and when he chooses!"

Professor Sciacca was of the same opinion.

"One thing is certain. At this moment, Don Nené is on the losing side. He's had to give way, as he did when he was forced to return the dossiers to Paolantonio, with the consequence that his four friends will be the first to go on trial! He's losing face."

"If you want my opinion, I think you should show a bit of patience."

"I've run out of patience. I've used it all up. Can you not see what he's made of? What the fuck did you get out of talking to him, eh, tell me that."

"I understand how he reasons. And that is, he doesn't reason at all."

"So?"

"I'm going back to Rome tomorrow, and I'll do what I can to have him transferred. That's why you'll need to show patience."

"And, in the meantime, he's going ahead with the four cases?"

"That's inevitable."

"Well, I'm going to make sure that it's not."

"Listen to me, Don Nené, and listen carefully. If you commit some fuck-up against the person of Judge Surra, not even Jesus Christ in person will be able to help you."

"I'll not lay a finger on your judge, so you can set off with an easy mind."

"So what are you going to do?"

"That's my damn business."

5

HE WAS WAKENED BY AN INSISTENT KNOCKING AT THE OUT-side door. Half-asleep, he peered into the early light of the morning and recognised Maresciallo Solano. Surra was alarmed.

"What's happened?"

"They've tried to set fire to the court. You'll have to come. I'll wait for you."

The news upset him so much that he found it hard to impose order on all the thoughts buzzing about in his head. He got dressed quickly and went downstairs.

"What's the situation now?"

"The fire was rapidly brought under control. Fortunately, the officer on watch saw the flames in time and raised the alarm."

"Is there much damage?"

"Not much, but your office has been partially destroyed. The green cabinet and the desk with all the papers they contained have been destroyed by the flames."

"Ah," the judge said, reassured. After a brief pause, he asked, "Why did you say it was arson?"

"Because to get in without being seen, they had to force open a side door."

In spite of the time, a group of about thirty bystanders had gathered in the space in front of the building.

One of them emerged from the crowd and approached the judge. He took off his hat.

It was Don Nené Lonero, displaying a solemnity of expression which befitted the occasion.

A sudden, tense silence fell on the square.

"I trust that justice has not suffered any serious reversal," he said.

"Justice has not suffered any reversal whatsoever, I can assure you," the judge replied with icy composure.

And he entered the court.

Proceeding along the corridor, he noted that the large black cupboard was intact and in its place.

It was impossible to get into his own office, which was completely blackened. Inside, Nicolosi and two clerks were busy picking over what little had been saved from the flames.

The green cabinet was reduced to a pile of ashes and pieces of charred wood, while half of the desk was simply no longer there.

"Where would you like to move to?" asked Nicolosi.

"To the office next door."

Many of the offices were still empty so there was no lack of choice.

He was joined by Judge Consolato.

"I just heard and I rushed over."

The judge gave him a smile. Madonna, that man must have steel wires where other men had nerves!

"Have you had any breakfast?"

"I didn't have time!"

"Nor did I. Want to come with me to the Caffè *Arnone?*"

"Glad to."

They went out and walked along the street together. Consolato summoned up the courage to break the silence.

"So it seems they broke in with the sole purpose of destroying the green cabinet."

"It looks that way, and they've succeeded totally."

Consolato yet again found himself admiring Surra's coolness and calm even in the face of a grave setback like this. Because it was obvious that there could be no possibility now of proceeding with the four cases.

They went into the caffè.

Don Nené Lonero was seated at a table with four of his men, pouring sparkling wine into glasses in front of them. Many other tables were occupied with people having their breakfast. On seeing Judge Surra enter, Don Nené rose to his feet, glass in hand. "Like to join us? Myself and my good friends Milioto, Savastano, Curreli and Costantino are celebrating."

The four men named stared at the judge, gave a bow and then burst out laughing. Those at the nearby tables joined in.

Consolato's face was grey. The judge remained impassive.

"No, thank you. I never drink in the morning." He turned to the barman and said. "What's that gentleman over there having?"

"A lemon *granita* and a *tarallo.*"

"I'd like to try that. What are you having, Consolato?"

"A . . . caff . . . caffelatte."

The judge consumed the *rigadi*. Every so often he closed his eyes.

"Good!" he said when he had finished it. "Will you bring me another?"

★ ★ ★

Since everyone on the court staff had rushed over as soon as they learned the news, Judge Surra was able to open the meeting an hour ahead of schedule. All around, he could see dark faces and furrowed brows. There was a funereal atmosphere.

He was about to start talking when Nicolosi came in to say that a correspondent of the *Giornale dell'Isola* would like to put a few questions to him on the attempted arson.

"Show him in," Surra said, to the surprise of the company.

"In here?" Nicolosi asked incredulously.

He was not the only one who was incredulous.

"Yes, in here."

The journalist came in, the judge sat him down and said: "I'm receiving you in the presence of my colleagues because my old office is out of commission and my new office is not yet ready for use."

"I won't take up much of your time," the journalist began. "I'm only seeking to confirm the facts—it's not my custom to publish inaccurate information. Is it true that a green cabinet in your office was completely destroyed?"

"Yes, and my desk too, come to that."

"There's a rumour in the town that that cabinet contained files and case notes of some importance. Can you confirm that?"

"I do confirm that."

"So I can write that the one motive of the people who broke into the court was to burn those documents?"

"I would say you could write that."

"And, in consequence, the damage done is irreparable?"

Judge Surra looked puzzled.

"Irreparable in what sense? Look, the desk had woodworm, the cabinet was in poor shape. I'll have new furniture purchased."

"I was referring to the papers which were inside."

"But those papers were no longer inside the cabinet," Surra said.

The entire company around the table simultaneously gave a start, causing the table around which they were seated to jump.

"They ... they weren't there anymore?" the journalist asked in wonderment.

"No, I'd taken them out and put them somewhere else."

He stared at his colleagues and they stared back at him. They saw in his eyes nothing but the candour of a snowfall on an Alpine peak.

"And then I forgot to mention that I'd moved them."

There was no need to wait for the arrival of the newspaper from Palermo the following day, because the news spread around Montelusa that very afternoon.

And curiously, here and there the town seemed to light up with sparks of sheer joy. There was laughter everywhere, in the houses, in the streets and in the bars. There was much winking and smiling, even among people who did not know one another.

"What finesse, what subtlety he employed to draw Don Nené into a deadly trap." Don Agatino Smecca had tears running down his cheeks from laughing too much and too long. For the occasion, he even switched to speaking Italian instead of dialect. "He prepared every move with infernal skill. First he showed the four files to the four judges and told them he would put them in the green cabinet, then he called the clerks and had them tidy them away, and then when they had all gone home, he took them out the cabinet and hid them somewhere else. The result was Don Nené's men burned an empty cabinet!"

"Excuse me," Professor Sciacca interrupted. "Why do you call it a deadly trap?"

"Because it's obvious that Don Nené is dead and buried in ridicule. It's a blow from which he can never recover. The judge has checkmated him. Lonero has lost all prestige, and he'll lose even more when the four judges get to work on the four files. Wait and see how many witnesses for the prosecution will find the courage to talk, strengthened by the presence of Judge Surra. How much are you going to bet that these trials will not end up with an acquittal on the grounds of insufficient evidence, as happens all too often in these parts?"

Don Agatino Smecca was a splendid prophet. A fortnight later, Don Nené Lonero let it be known that, for pressing family reasons, he was obliged to leave Montelusa and would move to Palermo, perhaps for good. The whisper was that Don Sabatino Vullo, a senior figure, a pair of steady hands and a man of vast experience, had been nominated in his place.

"Don't let anyone even think of asking me for favours regarding court matters while Judge Surra is in office," was the first declaration he made to his followers.

The judge himself remained for three years in charge of the Montelusa court, making it an example of efficiency, propriety and impartiality. His only relaxation was to go hunting every so often on his own. Attanasio had found him a good dog.

He was then recalled to Turin, where his wife found him somewhat overweight, and put him on a diet.

But memory of him lingered on in Montelusa for decades and decades. And when the court became once again less efficient, less scrupulous, less impartial and less transparent than he had wished and had made it, there were those who would sigh regretfully: "In the days of Judge Surra . . ."

I forgot one detail. The judge never did find the time to read the report by Don Pietro Ulloa which ex-President Fallarino had presented to him. Indeed, when he went back to Turin, he left it in Montelusa.

Translated by Joseph Farrell

Note

I quote here a passage from Don Pietro Ulloa's report which would undoubtedly have been of interest to Judge Surra, if he had read it.

There is not one public employee in Sicily who has not prostrated himself at the feet of some powerful figure and who has not considered taking advantage of his office. This general corruption has caused people to have recourse to certain, exceedingly strange and dangerous remedies. There are in many towns and villages Brotherhoods, who do not meet, who have no other link than subservience to a head who may be here a landowner or there a parish priest. A common fund provides for needs, perhaps to exonerate an official, perhaps to win him over, perhaps to protect an official or to convict an innocent party.

In other words, Judge Surra knew nothing of the existence of the Brotherhood, which was already known in his day as the "riga" and which somewhere along the way lost one "f."

The question is: had he known, would his attitude have been different?

We sincerely believe not.

We believe, on the contrary, that he preferred to remain in ignorance of its existence. He acted as though it were not there, and in so doing he unwittingly nullified it.

A.C.

Carlo Lucarelli

THE BAMBINA

1

HE ALWAYS MOVED HIS LIPS WHEN HE READ COMIC BOOKS.

Only comic books, because he was no great reader in any case and his secondary education only amounted to three years of vocational school, but he was not so backward that he had to sound out the sentences. He only did it with speech bubbles, and had done since he was little. It was his brother's fault.

His first comic was a Mickey Mouse book: *Mickey Mouse vs. Wolp, the Fearsome Bandit of the East.* Well, before that there were the strips in the *Corriere dei Piccoli*, but his mother had read the captions in those. Then he had started school, and just when he was learning to read, he and his brother had found the Mickey Mouse comic lying on the ground by the news stand— lucky for them, because there was no chance they would ever have been given fifty cents to buy it, with what his father earned as a policeman.

He was a year older than his brother, and got the first turn with the comic, but would not let it go, stumbling over all those new letters crammed into the little white bubbles, almost scraping them off the page with his lips before moving on to the next box. So Enrico, who unlike his brother read very quickly because he only looked at the pictures, had shouted "Get a move on!" and snatched it out of his hands.

Since then, even when they were older, he had continued to read sentence by sentence, word by word, murmuring under his breath, on purpose, to annoy his brother, who stubbornly refused to read the speech bubbles. "That way I can imagine what I want," Enrico told him, as he studied the drawings of Cino and Franco, Tarzan and Flash Gordon, always with a different expression on his face, as if he found something new in them every time. On the other hand, Ferro knew them off by heart after the third reading.

Then he had joined the police, following the family tradition, but for Enrico it was too late, because war broke out before he got the chance. He was sent to Albania and on to Russia before joining the partisans in the mountains, where he died.

So he carried on moving his lips even later on, as he read the adventures of Tex, the Little Sheriff, Kinowa, Tiramolla, Zagor and Comandante Mark, or the tales of Pedrito el Drito, Cristal and Billy Bis from *L'Intrepido* and *Il Monello*.

For a while he said he bought them for his children, even though they had grown older and had moved on to *Diabolik, Linus* and *Corto Maltese*. He had read those himself, even though he enjoyed them less, and always stubbornly moving his lips to the words. It was his way of remembering Enrico.

Now he was reading the special insert from a copy of *Lanciostory*, moving his lips to the adventures of a detective with a flattened, bloodhound's face just like his own. Even the moustache looked like his, but darker than the salt and pepper shade that made him look older than his fifty-six years. The Larry

Mannino story was taking him longer than usual, because first he had taken a look at the cover, and was stuck with two thoughts in his head. He knew that the trail for an interview with Pino Daniele would leave his song *Je so' pazzo* going round his head all day. And the drawing of a dark, suntanned girl in a bikini, with long black hair and an exotic ring round her ankle, had made him think of the seaside and brought a sudden longing for fried seafood. So he was reading about District 56 but dreaming of being in Riccione, with his wife, eating calamari and prawns with Pino Daniele playing in the background

"Ferro!"

He folded the comic in half lengthways and slipped it into his back pocket underneath his jacket, right next to the holster for his pistol. He got up from the car he had been leaning on and watched with interest as Grisenti approached, because he was not on his own. There was a younger officer with him, whose name escaped him.

"Change of plan."

"We're not going to pick up the judge?"

"I'm going with Mazzuca. You're being moved to another job."

"That's just not professional. How long have we been with the judge? Three months? We'd got used to Cancedda, but he," he said, pointing to the younger officer, "has to learn everything from scratch. It's unprofessional."

Mazzuca took a step backwards, holding up his hands as if to say it was not his fault.

"So what do they want me to do?"

"You're still looking after a judge. They've given you the Bambina."

"Me and who else?"

"No-one. It's just a safeguard. The Bambina doesn't need proper protection."

"Exactly."

Grisenti said no more. He opened the door, forcing Ferro to get up off the car, and climbed into the driver's seat. Mazzuca held up his hands again then got in.

They left him there in the middle of the car park at Bologna police headquarters wondering what was going on when after thirty-seven years on the force, someone like him, Brigadiere Ivano Ferrucci, known as Ferro, had to go and play taxi driver and porter to an examining magistrate who was so new and so young that everyone had nicknamed her "the little girl."

And while he was thinking this, somewhere inside his head he heard the silent voice of Pino Daniele.

While Ferro was fifty-six but looked older, the Bambina was thirty but looked younger. He knew how old she was because she had told him as soon as she got into the car—"Wish me many happy returns, today's my birthday. Born in 1950, I'm an old woman now!"—and he had counted back from 1 July, 1980. She was young enough to be his daughter—he even had a thirty-year-old daughter, the second of his three children. And it really did annoy him to be sat in the front of the station's unmarked Fiat Ritmo with that girl sitting in the back reading the paper. He looked like a driver taking his boss's daughter to university.

He looked at her in the rear-view mirror. Her lips were pressed together, slightly puckered in concentration, with a little frown line between her eyebrows and a handful of freckles round her nose, where her skin was flushed from the early July sunshine. Ferro had a bad hip, rheumatism and high blood pressure, but his vision was as good as ever, especially his eye for detail, which he noticed instinctively. He had noted her flat shoes, skirt, white blouse, black sweater and the denim jacket over one shoulder as soon as she had introduced herself when he picked her up from her house—"Valentina Lorenzini, pleased to meet you." Short hair down to her shoulders, blond, fastened at the back with a tortoiseshell comb. Pretty, dainty—a cute little thing.

An examining magistrate at Bologna Law Court, first posting. The Bambina.

"Do you mind?"

The Bambina reached forward between the two seats, with a waft of Camay soap and apple shampoo, the same as his daughter used. She used a finger to press the ON button on the stereo, then leant further forward to flick through the radio's pre-programmed stations. The muffled voice of Pino Daniele came out of the speaker under the dashboard.

"Just a second, Dottoressa . . . would you mind leaving this one please?"

The Bambina went back to her seat.

"You like Pino Daniele?"

"No, but I've had it in my head all morning . . . If I can listen to the song, it'll go." He sighed as he felt the music melting away in his head, setting him free. "Shall I change it?" he said, at last.

"No, it's fine. It's not what I usually listen to but it's fine. Mind if I have a look?"

She picked up the copy of *Il Resto del Carlino* that Ferro had left on the passenger's seat, but dropped the newspaper immediately when she saw the gun underneath.

"Oh God!"

"Sorry. I put it there because I wear it behind my back, but when I'm driving . . ."

"I think you could keep it behind your back if you want. I don't think you'll ever need to use it with me."

"You never know . . ."

"What do you mean, you never know?"

She laughed, and Ferro smiled as well. The Bambina touched the metal pillar beside the Ritmo's window for luck, and he quickly made the sign of the horns between his legs while she was not looking.

"Judges working on political investigations need bodyguards, like poor Mario Amato, the one they killed at the tram stop. As far as I'm concerned, I could carry on riding my scooter to court. Do you know what I'm doing this morning?"

She picked up the newspaper, uncovering the pistol again, but it seemed not to bother her any more. Opening it up, she flicked through to the middle pages.

"See, it's not even in there."

She folded it shut and stopped to look at the photograph of the airplane on the front page. Underneath was the horrible, grainy shot of the dead bodies in the sea off the island of Ustica, white blotches on the black water, people floating belly-up like fish.

"And that's why," she murmured, "There's more serious news than my fraudulent bankruptcy."

They had reached the court. Ferro got out of the car and walked round to open the door for her, but the Bambina had already got out.

"See you this evening," she said, waving a hand in the air as he watched her walk off, so blond and tiny, with her denim jacket and briefcase slung over one shoulder, thinking that without the pistol under his newspaper and the carabinieri squad car parked outside the court, he really could have been a driver taking his boss's daughter to university.

But that evening, when he went to pick her up, she had changed. She was still tiny, still the Bambina, but for a moment, when she stopped at the court door, lost in thought and looking off into the distance, she really did look like a woman who had just turned thirty.

She left Ferro with his hand on the back door and got into the front, sitting down in the passenger's seat, then kicked off her shoes and rested her feet on the dashboard, curling her knees up against her chest.

"Do you mind?" she asked, and Ferro didn't know whether she was talking about her feet or the seat, but then he saw the cassette in her hand and nodded. She put it into the stereo, pressed fast forward until she found the song she was looking for, then turned up the volume, leaning her head back on the seat, with her eyes closed.

The speaker in the unmarked Ritmo was pretty clapped out and vibrated on the bass line that beat like an ageing heart, whereas the drumming was just an intermittent scraping sound, like someone blowing through their lips. Far off, almost like an echo, you could hear the singing. The Bambina turned up the volume even higher.

"Do you like it?" she said, without opening her eyes.

"It's a bit too gloomy for me . . . My son would like it."

"I'll turn it off as soon as this one's over. It calms me down."

"Bad day?"

"I don't know. Maybe, maybe not. Do you like your job?"

"I do. Family tradition, my dad was a policeman, my granddad was a policeman . . . I'll be retiring in a couple of years."

"Me too . . . The family tradition, I mean, not that I'm about to retire. My father was a judge, but I didn't go into it for him. This evening though, I don't know whether to love the job or hate it. But I'll think about it tomorrow, today's my birthday."

"How are you going to celebrate?"

"With my cat, Cointreau on the rocks and a long chat to my boyfriend on the phone—he's a lawyer in Turin. And The Cure," she added, pointing to the stereo, before closing her eyes again, immersing herself in that faraway, dark music.

She lived in Casalecchio, and by the time they got there, they had already heard another two tracks because she was so tied up in her thoughts that she had forgotten her promise to turn off the tape. She slipped on her shoes, picking them up off the floor with her feet, and turned around to pick up the bag she had left on the back seat. That was when the shadow moved.

Ferro had already seen it and realised it wasn't a shadow, but a man emerging from behind a van parked by the kerb. He had seen the gun even before the man stretched out his arm towards the Ritmo's windscreen. He immediately reached out to grab his Beretta from the seat, but then stopped and reached round towards his back, but with the seat, the jacket and his position, he was too late.

The first shot shattered the windscreen and brought a cry of pain from the Bambina, short like a sob, the second made her body jolt, and the third was meant for him, but in the meantime he had managed to open the door and throw himself out. His age, his hip, his rheumatism and even his high blood pressure vanished immediately as he drew his gun, flicked off the safety catch and let off as many shots as he could. He carried on shooting at the van as it pulled away with a squeal of tyres, holding the pistol with two hands and squeezing the trigger with his finger, until the slide shot back for the last time, leaving him with no more rounds to fire.

If she had not turned round to get her bag from the back seat, she would have been killed. Judging from the position of the .38-calibre bullet holes on the back of the seat, at least one round would have torn through her heart. Instead, the first had cut a long slice across her back like a blade, and the second had hit her in the side, between her ribs, without killing her or hitting any vital organs, but leaving her hanging between life and death, in a drug-induced coma at the Ospedale Maggiore.

They all said it wasn't his fault, but he knew that some of them thought it was—that Ferro had lost it, that age was taking its toll and he'd almost let the judge get killed on his watch, and it didn't even matter if no-one thought like that, because he did.

Even though he was O.K., they had given him two days off sick. He spent the first in and out of the station, buzzing with adrenalin and unable to rest. Had anyone claimed responsibility? No. Identikit matches? No. Arrested anyone? No. Go home, Ferro, we're handling it.

He only asked for news about the Bambina at the end of the day, afraid they would tell him that the operation had gone badly, there had been complications, she had died. And he asked not at the hospital, but at work, as if talking to a colleague could lessen the fear of hearing bad news.

On the second day he collapsed and stayed at home, doing practically nothing but watch television. He sat there until *L'Almanacco del giorno dopo* came on, with its whistling soundtrack and title sequence of prints scrolling across the screen, like the ones on *Carosello*. According to the Almanac, tomorrow was July 4, the sun would rise at 5:40 a.m. and set at 8:49 p.m., the moon would rise at 12:56 a.m. and set at 12:18 p.m., and tomorrow's saints were Elizabeth of Portugal and Ulrich of Augsburg. The historical section was dedicated to Giovanni Papini, and the language section to the phrases "at loggerheads" and "putting your cards on the table."

Then, at the end, the old man with the scythe and the flag, THE SHOW IS OVER.

He missed the motto of the day, and all the rest.

That was the signal for dinner time. He went through to the kitchen to see steaks frying in the pan and his wife draining the pasta. Only two places were laid.

"Isn't Lorenzo eating?"

"He says he's not feeling well."

"I can't remember the last time he did feel well."

Lorenzo had come late, out of the blue. Annalaura and Giovanna were born straight away, as soon as he had started to sort himself out after the war, but then their son had arrived seventeen years later, just like that. Now he was eighteen and since he had come back from his trip to London, a reward for passing his exams, he always dressed in black, with a ridiculous haircut, short at the back and hanging down over his face. Dressed like a fascist with screwed-up hair, Ferro liked to say, but Lorenzo replied in disgust that it had nothing to do with politics. That was something, at least—he wasn't involved with some bunch of right-wing or left-wing activists. As for drugs, he was less sure. When Lorenzo was out, he carefully searched his room, making sure to be discreet, but had never found anything.

He left the kitchen, paying no attention to his wife's plea to "leave him alone," which was delivered in a resigned monotone in any case. Two steps down the corridor and he was standing in front of the closed door to Lorenzo's bedroom. He put his hand on the doorknob but stopped, hearing a familiar beat from the other side of the laminated wood. He opened the door.

Lorenzo was stretched out on the bed, with his hands behind his shaved neck, looking at the ceiling. He lowered his eyes to look at his father, and tensed up, shrinking back defensively, ready for a row. But Ferro was looking at the shiny record spinning on the Sony turntable, a present from his sisters, also for the exams.

"Is that The Cure?"

Lorenzo shrank back even further, as if he had been hit. His father had said "the kyoor" with the hard "u" and long "r" of someone repeating something they had heard, but he had still got the name of his favourite band right.

"Yes," Lorenzo said, sitting up on the bed, "but how did . . ."

"Come on, let's have some dinner."

At the dinner table, Lorenzo asked him again, "How come you've heard of The Cure?," and then Ferro told him about the Bambina, as his wife looked on in surprise, because it had been a long time since those two had talked, and she almost burned the steaks when she realised that a bit of Lorenzo's admiration for the judge who listened to the same music as he did had rubbed off on his policeman father.

After dinner, Ferro went out. He took the car and drove to the Ospedale Maggiore, went in through the emergency department, showing his I.D. card, and up to the wards. The door to Intensive Care was shut, and he was about to ring the bell, but in the meantime a nurse arrived, opening the door for herself and letting him through as well, seeing as he was a policeman.

Lo Iacono was at the end of the corridor, sitting on a metal chair with his legs apart as if he was on the toilet. He was twirling his cap on the end of his finger. They knew each other, so he recognised Ferro immediately.

"There's someone from the police who wants to see you downstairs," the nurse said to Lo Iacono, who looked at Ferro.

"Don't worry, I'll be here."

He waited for his colleague and the nurse to leave, not wanting them to see him take a deep breath to steady himself. Hospitals had always frightened him. The smell, that acid smell of disinfectant and medicine, always made him feel weak, turned his flesh to jelly.

When he opened the door and put his head into the room, he could barely see the Bambina. There was a bed and an I.V. tube running under the sheets, and she was in there too, but seeing her so small and thin, as white as the pillow, with her legs hidden in the folds of the bedclothes, Ferro let out a sigh of despair and pity that came out of his throat with a painful rasp. Her eyes were closed and she was breathing lightly but regularly through her mouth, in time with the humming of another machine attached to her by more tubes on the other side of the bed.

Ferro gritted his teeth, tears stinging his eyes. He moved over to the window and looked outside, trying to convince himself that her regular breathing and the lack of any other noises from the machine meant that everything was alright. Thinking that when the nurse came back with Lo Iacono, he would ask her: "Everything's O.K., isn't it?"

Intensive Care was in a fairly tall building with a view of the street. Ferro was looking out distractedly, lost in his own thoughts, but all the same he caught sight of Lo Iacono out there, bending down to talk to someone through the window of a black car. Then Lo Iacono stood up, bringing his hand up to the peak of his cap in a salute, and walked off towards the car park. Ferro still noticed all this, even as he was trying to forget that rasping sigh.

Policeman's instinct.

"Changing shift," he said to himself, but then he thought "No." It's nine o'clock and the shifts run from midnight to six, six to midday, midday to six and six to midnight. He had done guard duty so many times himself.

He watched Lo Iacono disappear into the dusky summer evening, wondering why he felt so uneasy. There could be millions of explanations. Someone could have decided to stop surveillance at the hospital, a relief shift could be on the way after all, perhaps the carabinieri had taken over, or the danger had passed, but in that case why did he feel so tense, standing there with his forehead pressed against the window watching that black car, which hadn't moved?

Policeman's instinct.

Then he saw them emerge from the shadows of the car park. They walked past the black car, and the largest of the three slapped his hand on the bonnet in a sort of greeting. Three men, in plain clothes, wearing jeans and casual jackets. Were they carabinieri? No, because the third, the thinnest one, stopped for a moment to light up a cigarette. He seemed agitated and turned his head upwards to take the first drag, so Ferro saw him clearly, illuminated by the hospital's yellow light.

He was the one from the identikit.

The man who had shot at him.

Ferro moved back, away from the window, as if the other man could see him. He instinctively fished under his jacket for his pistol. For a moment he thought about going out, calling someone, calling 113, but he didn't want to leave the Bambina on her own and he couldn't get help from the doctors and nurses—he was in a hospital, not a police station. The only telephone he remembered seeing was downstairs, and they were down there.

He locked the door and trained his gun on it. But that was no good either. Even if he started shooting, they would be able to get in and kill both of them before anyone who could help could get to them.

To his left was a bathroom. The door was open and you could see another closed door leading into another room. Ferro shook the handle, then planted a kick with the sole of his shoe flat against the door, bracing himself against the basin, and broke the lock. The other room was dark and empty.

Ferro went back to the Bambina and stopped by the bed, suffering a sudden moment of weakness. All those tubes and needles, and her so thin and pale. For a moment, he felt himself starting to black out, then pulled himself together, took the tube out of the drip bag, because he could not bring himself to touch the needle, and pulled the tubes out of the machine. Trying to remember picking up his first daughter just after she was born, when she was so small he was afraid of breaking her, he slid his hands under the sheets and picked up the Bambina. She weighed nothing.

He went through the bathroom, closing the first door behind him, and stood motionless in the dark room, holding his breath. He heard them come into the Bambina's room, and one of them saying: "Where the fuck . . ." Then he went out into the empty corridor and over to the lift, which was still waiting with its doors open.

It seemed to take forever to go down. For what seemed like an eternity, he looked at himself in the mirror, holding the pale, limp little girl in his arms, barefoot and dressed only in the light hospital gown, with the tubes coming out of her arms like plastic tentacles. What was he doing? For all he knew, he might just have killed her. Then the endless wait was over, the lift doors opened, and Ferro ran out.

"Call 113!" he shouted to the nurse staring wide-eyed at him, and carried on running because he knew they were already coming down.

He wanted to get to his car in the car park, but the black car was in front of the building. A man got out of the driver's seat and leant on the roof. Ferro could see he was taking aim. He would never have let go of the Bambina, so he fired his weapon from under her. The bullet went through the open windows and threw the man backwards onto a flowerbed.

Another shot, from behind. Ferro didn't hear it but saw it slam into the car door. He didn't even turn around to see the men shooting at him, just threw the Bambina into the back and ran

round to the driver's seat. Without the silencers that made their
shots so inaccurate, they would already have hit him. Instead,
another bullet hit one of the car's windscreen pillars and one
whistled past his nose, like a hornet. Then he managed to get the
car into gear and skidded away.

He joined the Via Emilia and drove, trying to work out which
direction he was heading. He had planned to go straight to the
station and carry the Bambina inside in his arms, but then he
started to think, or rather a feeling came over him. A feeling of
unease mixed with agitation and fear—he had shot and been
shot at—but something different as well, something more lucid
and cold.

Policeman's instinct.

He slowed down and stopped at the red light he had planned
to jump. Looking around the car, he saw the dashboard modi-
fied to hold the police radio, with the microphone hanging
from its coiled wire, and the red and white signalling disk stuck
behind the passenger's sun visor. On the seat next to him was
the jacket belonging to the man he had shot. He squeezed the
fabric with his hand until he felt something in the inside pocket.
It was a wallet with an identity card. Maresciallo Montana of the
carabinieri.

The light turned green again, but Ferro didn't move. There
was no-one behind him. Screaming sirens sped down the Via
Emilia, in the opposite direction. He turned on the radio, and
quickly tuned into the right frequency, where he heard a description of the car, as well as a very accurate description of himself,
missing only the name.

They were saying he had abducted an examining magistrate
and killed a maresciallo in the carabinieri.

The first name that came to mind was Grisenti: "He can help
me, we'll talk to Judge Cancedda . . ." He had to find a phone box,

or go straight back home. Then he heard a moan from the back, and remembered about the Bambina. She was curled up on the seat, with her eyes closed and those plastic tentacles, looking paler than ever. On her side, under the hospital gown, a dark shadow had spread, making him go weak again.

There was no more time to think. That cold feeling of dread was stopping him from going straight to the station or calling 113, and there was no way he could take her back to the hospital and guard her with his gun drawn until someone he could trust got there. What if the other lot turned up? If he was arrested as soon as he showed his face? But there was no more time.

That was when he thought of the second name, put the car into gear and pulled away, even though the light was still red.

The other name was Sanna. He lived in Croce di Casalecchio, in an isolated little house almost out in the countryside, even though it was next to the ring road. He was already in bed, and when he saw Ferro through the window he closed the curtains and turned out the light, but Ferro started hammering on the glass with an open hand, hard enough to break it.

"What do you want?"

"I need some help."

"Why, have you been hurt?"

"I haven't, but she has."

Clutching his pyjamas tight around his neck, Sanna came out to look into the back of the car.

"Shit," he said, "who is she?"

"An examining magistrate."

Sanna took a step backwards, still looking at the Bambina.

"Are you fucking joking?" he said. "I've been arrested three times for illegally practicing medicine and now a policemen turns up and wants me to take care of a judge?"

In the basement of Sanna's house was a perfectly equipped clinic, showing that he had gone back to sewing up gangsters injured in fire fights with the police. In the fridge he had packs of blood—he had clearly been busy recently—and even a machine like the one in the hospital next to the bed he used for surgery.

When your adrenaline levels plummet—as Ferro knew—the next stage is extreme tiredness, but going to sleep would certainly not have been a good idea. He waited for Sanna to deal with the Bambina, seeing him nod quietly, which meant that everything was going well for now, then left and drove to a phone box far enough away. He felt slow, with his head full of a buzzing fog that made his movements drag. He put the token Sanna had given him into the slot and would have fallen asleep on his feet, with his forehead resting on the cold metal of the telephone, if his wife had not picked up immediately.

"No, no, don't worry, everything's fine, nothing's happened … I'm going to be out all night working though … No, don't worry, I'll tell you about it tomorrow … Yes, the judge is fine. Bye, bye."

Was that a metallic click he'd heard while he was talking to his wife? Had he done the right thing not phoning from Sanna's house? Or was it just the paranoia that develops when people have tried to kill you twice? He tried not to think about the man he had shot. It had happened before, at the beginning of his career, and he knew how to deal with it.

So he went back to the car, rested the back of his neck on the seat back, hooked his hands over the steering wheel to relax his arms. *Just a minute, only a minute, besides, it's dangerous to stay here in this car.* Then he closed his eyes and went to sleep.

When he woke it was almost morning. He rubbed his face with his hands, got out of the car and walked around the neighbourhood, looking for a bar that was open. He found one where they were just opening the shutters, and while the barman warmed up the coffee machine, he asked for another token and went to make a phone call behind the pinball machines, which were still turned off.

Grisenti took a while to answer, probably because he was still in bed.

"It's Ferro . . . I know, calm down, I know they're all looking for me . . . Forget about the Bambina . . . Let me get a word in, Christ! I'll come to the station, but I want you and the judge to be there. I'll tell you the whole story, I'll tell you everything, don't worry . . . Yes, I know you'll have to arrest me, look, I'll put the handcuffs on myself, you can arrest me, but you have to let me talk to Cancedda, O.K.? You've got to listen to me . . . Don't worry about the Bambina, she's fine, I saved her life . . . No, I won't tell you where she is, I'll tell you when I get there . . . Go and get the judge and go to the station. Bye."

He hung up, thinking that this time he hadn't heard a click, but that didn't mean anything, then went to drink his coffee.

"What do you expect," the bartender said, seeing him pull a face, "it's the first of the day. We shouldn't even be open yet."

He wanted to give Grisenti enough time to get to the station with the judge and also check on the Bambina, so he went back to Sanna's place on the first bus of the morning. She was fine, sleeping in the little surgical bed, with the drip in her arm and the machine on the other side, just as it had been in the hospital. Instead of the blood-stained gown, she was wearing a pair of Sanna's striped pyjamas. She even seemed to have regained a bit of colour.

The coffee from Sanna's moka pot was better than the stuff from the bar. Ferro had started to tell him a bit about what had happened, but the doctor had stopped him without a word, just holding up his hand. Ferro nodded, finished his coffee and left.

To get to the station, he had called a taxi, getting the driver to pick him up on the corner. As they drove through Bologna, Ferro thought that he had always liked the city at that time of the morning. It reminded him of a woman stretching before getting out of bed, all soft and sensual. When he was on Flying Squad duty and coming back from a night shift, he always made one more circuit to enjoy the morning light still sparkling in the moist air, and the way the sounds were amplified, ringing out suddenly before dissolving into the quietness left over from the night.

There was no way he could ask the taxi driver to carry on to the Two Towers then turn around just so he could enjoy his beloved Bologna—there was no time—so he let him turn into Via della Zecca and got out in Piazza Roosevelt, just in time to see Grisenti and Mazzuca getting out of the car with Judge Cancedda.

Ferro raised a hand above his head to wave, but didn't manage to say anything.

He heard Grisenti shout "Watch out!" and saw the white van coming up behind him out of the corner of his eye. There was no pain when it rear-ended him, just a sudden irritation that made him curl his lip as he heard his hip bone break like a stick of wood. There would have been plenty of pain a moment later, but he didn't feel it because, in the meantime, he had flipped over, smashing the windscreen with the back of his neck, and was dead even before he slid off the bonnet onto the street.

2

VALENTINA OPENED HER EYES WITH THE FEELING THAT IT
was not the first time, even though she could not remember
how or when. It was not the low ceiling with the patch of damp
that looked like a dolphin, or the low-rent hospital furnishings,
or even the man asleep on the armchair, with one leg slung over
the armrest and his cheek resting on his hand. She had the feeling she had seen him before—a dark, skinny man with a thin
moustache and what looked like a dentist's white jacket—but he
was not the source of her familiar feeling of déjà vu.

It was the music, the voice that was too smooth for her tastes,
the way the singer stretched out the end of each word, rising and
falling over the lively rhythm and the strumming of the guitar,
distorted by the speaker of a little portable radio.

Valentina sat up on the bed, abruptly, grabbing onto the edges
when the dizziness hit her. She would have fallen if the man had
not jumped down from the chair to support her.

"Careful, careful!"

He tried to lay her back down but Valentina resisted, grabbing onto his neck like a monkey because she had no strength in her back.

"O.K., O.K.," the man whispered, "stay sitting, but I'll hold you."

It was only then that she noticed the pyjamas and the drip tube and also the pain in her side that burned as if the flesh had been torn, and at that point she felt so weak that she pulled down on the man's neck with her arms, making him lower her back down onto the bed.

She kept her eyes closed for a few moments, breathing through her mouth, not so much because of the pain or fatigue, which were subsiding, but more to get her thoughts in order, to sort out the jumble of questions that were building up in her head, which hurt even more than the wound in her side. She had to use what she had learnt when she was training, when she used to note down the sequence of the prosecutors' questions.

"Where am I?"

She had wondered whether she would be able to talk. In fact, all that emerged was a rasp from the back of her parched throat, so hoarse that Sanna only understood the question because he was expecting it. He had spent the last two days wondering what to say when the judge who looked like a little girl opened her eyes.

"Wait," he said, holding up her head so she could drink from the glass bottle he held up to her lips.

"Where am I?" Valentina repeated.

"In a clandestine hospital."

Valentina let the mineral water tickle her throat as it slipped down. His reply had opened up a whole horizon of new questions.

"Are you a doctor?"

"I was. Struck off ten years ago. Clandestine hospital, clandestine doctor."

Valentina did not smile, and neither did Sanna. It was not a joke.

"Why am I here?"

"Because you were shot."

"And why not a proper hospital?"

"Because they tried to kill you there as well. Don't ask me any more, I didn't want to know. Ferro brought you here."

Valentina closed her eyes and took a deep breath. She grasped the edge of the bed and sat upright again, because she could not think while lying down like that. She was less dizzy now, and only needed to lean on Sanna's shoulder for a moment to regain her balance.

Ferro's name was the key. It helped her to piece together her life, everything that had happened before she had turned round to get her bag in the car. Everything in its place, in order.

"How long have I been here?"

"Three days. And before that three days in hospital, the real one. More or less in a coma the whole time, apart from the last two days when you were only sedated. By me."

"And how am I doing?"

"Better."

"You said Ferro brought me here? You mean Brigadiere Ferrucci?"

"That's right, Ferro."

"And where is he?"

"He's dead."

Valentina looked down. She stretched out one bare foot towards the floor, but could not reach. She rubbed her feet together, pressing them one against the other like hands. The picture was starting to come into focus. Confused, hypothetical, based on suppositions, but things were starting to point in a certain direction. A direction she didn't like. There was so much more she needed to know: how Ferro had died, why, what was going on out there. But first she had to ask another question. She needed to know about the tiny, restless man in the white dentist's jacket.

"Why did you keep me here? You could have left me outside a hospital, or somewhere else and called the carabinieri."

Sanna shrugged.

"Hippocratic oath," he said, and Valentina was unsure whether it was a joke, because Sanna's lips only moved slightly, and it was difficult to tell if the face he pulled was a smile.

One of the questions Valentina wanted to ask was about the song that was still playing. Why did she feel like she had heard it so many times before? Then she worked it out herself, just as Sanna switched off the radio, saying that it had really helped her to come out of her coma. The song had to be the big hit of the summer: "Luna." It carried on bouncing around her head for a while, annoying and incomplete.

Sanna had bought her a newspaper that she was unable to read, so he read it to her out loud. The examining magistrate assigned to the case was suggesting that Brigadiere Ferrucci had been tormented by the idea that he had been unable to protect her, so he had kidnapped her and hidden her somewhere. Then, regretting his actions, he had contacted his colleagues, but was so disturbed that he walked out into the road like a madman and had ended up under a van. The story gave the name of the examining magistrate. Valentina knew him and had always thought he was an idiot.

On the subject of her attack, initially they had thought it was an act of terrorism, or at least something to do with her investigations, but this theory had been rejected, because she was only looking into an ordinary case of bankruptcy. Valentina had frowned when she heard that the main suspect in her inquiries, the owner of the company, had disappeared right after being questioned, and now they were saying he must be enjoying the money in Barbados.

Then she found out that the new theory was a crime of passion. In Turin, they were questioning her boyfriend, whilst waiting for the ballistics report on a pistol found in his apartment.

"Roberto? That's ridiculous," she said.

Sanna's lips moved and this time you could see it was a smile. He was amused by the fact that the young judge was still sedated enough to react to everything that was happening to her with Herculean calm. They had tried to kill her, killed her bodyguard and arrested her boyfriend, and she described it as "ridiculous," sitting there on the armchair in her pyjamas, as if she had just got out of bed and was reading a film review.

He was calm too, but only because he had learned to stay relaxed. Otherwise he would have killed someone by now. Like when he was at university and saw all the little rich boys beat him in the exams, and then when he applied for jobs, and at the hospital, in Cagliari, until they caught him treating a fugitive in the mountains, a friend of a friend, because he was in no position to say no, and didn't even want to. As a clandestine doctor, and then an underworld doctor, it had not been easy to cultivate the relaxed and amenable attitude of someone at peace with the world and society. Or perhaps, who knows, he was just anxious, tense and angry by nature.

The last thing that Sanna had read to her was that they were looking everywhere for her.

"I have to call the police, or the carabinieri, or someone . . ."

"I'd think carefully about that . . ."

"I won't turn you in. I should, but I don't even know where I am. And I don't know your name."

"Not for my sake, for yours. One of the few things that Ferro did tell me was about carabinieri who weren't exactly carabinieri. People who could make police guards disappear, smooth operators . . . so I don't know if you can really trust everyone on your side."

"I have to trust them, I'm a judge."

Sanna spread out his arms and shrugged. Valentina closed her eyes, sinking her head back into the cushion on the chair. Even though she felt as if there was a cloud inside her head, she could still think clearly. Carabinieri who aren't exactly carabinieri, or policemen who aren't exactly policemen, meant the secret services. And sometimes rogue elements of the secret services.

"Sometimes?" Sanna asked, and Valentina realised she had been talking out loud.

"Sometimes," she repeated. "The picture keeps getting clearer. Certain things happened before I got shot . . ."

"I don't want to know."

"I was investigating a fraudulent bankruptcy."

"I don't want to know."

"And it turned out that a certain accountant owned a company—"

"I don't want to know!"

He had not shouted, he never did. It was a growl. His fists were clenched, and Valentina thought for a moment he was going to hit her. Instead he stuffed them into the pockets of his jacket, pushing them right down so that they stretched the fabric.

"I'm hungry," Valentina said.

"I can imagine," Sanna replied, "you've been surviving on the drip for a week."

"Can I eat?"

"You can do all kinds of things. Your condition's not as bad as it seems. You could even go. I could leave you at a phone box, so you could . . ."

"No. I'm a judge, an examining magistrate, and there are two things I have to do. One is to trust the system. You're part of the underworld, but I'm not, I'm part of the system. And it's my job to defend it and keep it healthy."

Who had said that? Her professor at university?

"Well then, put your trust in it. Call 113."

"No. I do trust the system, but not blindly like that. When judges know too much but still don't have anything concrete, they end up getting killed. You see it in the news, and I'm not just talking about me. If things are the way I think they are, I might not have enough protection."

"And the second thing?"

"What?"

"You said there were two things you have to do. The first is to put your faith in the system, and the second?"

"Investigate. I can't just let it drop and pretend nothing happened. Was the brigadier a friend of yours?"

"Ferro? No."

It was true, in a way. Ferro was fair, loyal and likeable, a good guy, someone he liked enough to become friends with, in other circumstances, but people like him didn't make friends with the law.

"I only met him twice, for a few minutes, in the car. But it makes me sick that they killed him like that. Because he was killed, right? We're certain of that."

Sanna swallowed, clenching his fists in his pockets. It made him sick too.

"What happened to Ferro would be enough, but it's not just about him. Yesterday evening . . . no, a week ago, I was wondering why I did my job, well now I know why. I was investigating . . . No, let me tell you," Sanna had held up a hand, but Valentina leant forward, gripping the arms of the chair, "then you can forget again if you want, but let me tell you. I was investigating a fraudulent bankruptcy, an accountant who made a load of money disappear from his company through a series of shell companies, putting a hell of a lot of people on the streets in the process, and it made me really, really angry, because there are people like him who do what they like, who don't give a shit about the rules, and all these people are left behind who've lost everything, because they put their trust in them. Well, that makes me angry."

Sanna gave a little nod. It made him angry as well.

"When I investigated, I discovered that in this kaleidoscope of imaginary companies, there was one with links to the secret services. So rather than embezzlement, this bankruptcy seems to have been a botched attempt to gather illegal funds."

Valentina had stood up without noticing, so caught up in her argument that her head was not even spinning. She still had a hand on the back of the armchair, but she was pacing back and forth, barefoot and in her pyjamas, with her tousled hair brushing against her shoulders. She really did look like a little girl.

"So I went to my boss and told him what I suspected, but he wasn't convinced. In fact, he told me that I didn't have the experience for this sort of thing and he was bringing in an older colleague to support me, the idiot who said those ridiculous things about Ferro. And then they tried to kill me."

Valentina caught her breath. She put a hand on her side, over the dressing covering her wound, which was throbbing annoyingly.

"I'd be suspicious," Sanna said.

"Me too," Valentina said, "but that's not really the point. If it's really about secret funds and rogue factions of the secret service, it pisses me off even more. People who go over our heads and decide what's best. Best for them, of course . . . and then they do things behind our backs and don't give a shit if someone gets caught in the middle and gets killed. Well, I'm not standing for it. That's why I'm a judge and that's why I can't let it go."

Valentina sank back down onto the chair, with her elbow on the armrest and her chin in her hand. Her lips pursed in a thoughtful, determined expression. The other hand resting on her side and her bare feet one on top of the other.

The Law personified.

The Law in pyjamas.

Valentina looked up at Sanna. The frown of concentration between her eyebrows relaxed, but not much. There was still a steely look of determination in her eyes

"I'm going to ask you for three things. I'd like something to wear and something to eat, please—I'm dying of hunger. And the third thing . . . I'll tell you afterwards."

Sanna nodded, thinking to himself: "That's the Law, a girl in her pyjamas," and at that moment, he knew for certain he would do whatever she asked.

There were only two places in Bologna where you could get pastis to compare to those made in Marseille. Because it is not just about mixing water and Pernod—which even then would not be a real pastis, though it comes to the same thing—you need the right water and the right spirit and the right hand and the right atmosphere. Basically, you need Marseille.

He had gone to Marseille for a couple of years after being struck off, when it almost looked like he was going to go to prison. A brother-in-law who was a lawyer had kept him out of jail, but in France he had specialised in patching up gangsters with gunshot wounds, and only when it looked like he might end up inside over there as well, had he come back to Italy. Bologna had seemed anarchic enough, underneath it all, and over the past five years he had had second thoughts and then convinced himself all over again, at least a dozen times.

But Bologna was Bologna, not Marseille, and he could only get a Pernod that would almost hit the spot at an *osteria* in Pratello, where the owner was from Marseille, and a little bar in Pilastro, God knows why.

The *osteria* made a better drink than the bar, but Pilastro was more down at heel than Pratello and he didn't want to be seen by the wrong people. In that hole on the edge of town, amongst the little concrete low-rises like beehives, the police almost never came round. And when they did, everyone knew about it straight away.

The bar had no tables outside, just chairs with plastic slats that had been white once upon a time. Sanna sat down in the setting sun, under the metal canopy, with his glass resting on one knee. He always wore his shirt buttoned up, but he undid the collar because the early July heat was oppressive that year, and the sultry humidity brought you out in a sweat.

It had not taken much to convince the Ricciuti brothers to help him, far from it. They owed him plenty of favours. Or rather one of them did, the younger one, who used to be an armed robber and had been shot by security guards a couple of times. Now he had teamed up with his elder brother, turning over apartments and breaking into safes, but a hip fractured by a 9mm bullet still gave him trouble, and Sanna got him prescriptions for painkillers under the counter and free of charge.

But if he had told them who they were working for and why, he might not have been able to convince them even with a debt of honour. Especially the way Valentina had put it.

"Now I've gone underground just like you—an underground examining magistrate. So I'll run an underground investigation. I'd uncovered the alleged headquarters of one of the accountant's companies and I was about to ask the finance police to do a search. So I'm asking you to do it instead: an underground search."

All her underground this, that and the other would not have been enough to hide the fact that they were doing police work. And working for the law, even if she was a girl in striped pyjamas.

He finished his pastis and pushed his chair back, because the sun was going down fast and hurting his eyes where it shone under the edge of the canopy. The Ricciutis said this was the best time to turn over an office. After the workers have gone home and before the night watchmen start doing their rounds. The office was almost empty, besides, so it would be a quick job. In fact, they should have been back already.

A kid went by on a bicycle, ringing his bell as if to clear the way, but there was no-one in front of him. Sanna got up from his chair and went into the bar, ordering another pastis as he waited for the carabinieri to drive slowly past and disappear round the corner. He went back to his seat and sipped at the whitish liquid clouding the glass.

What about him? Why was he helping one of them? Or rather, why was he obeying this girl? Since she had explained everything whilst devouring four scrambled eggs, he had almost been standing to attention, taking orders as if he really was a maresciallo in the finance police.

Why? For Ferro? For her, because she was a pretty, delicate little thing with those cute freckles? He had already seen her naked when he had undressed her to tend her wounds, and dressed her again afterwards. He had even touched her, when she was just a patient in a coma, but then she became a woman again, warm from the bed, dressed in rumpled pyjamas.

Or because he too didn't like them doing whatever they wanted behind people's backs and over their heads?

There was no time to come up with an answer, because the Ricciutis had arrived in their car and driven round the back of the bar to the car park. Only the older one got out. The younger one was in the back, and from the awkward way he was sitting, Sanna could see he had taken another bullet.

"What happened?"

He was about to go over to the younger brother, but the older one stopped him with a hand on his shoulder.

"Later. It's not serious and he's used to it. Take a look at this."

He glanced around to check that no-one was around, but the car park was empty. Then he opened the boot to reveal a man curled up in a foetal position, with his hands and feet tied and a purple bruise between his closed eyes.

"Good thing that fucking office was supposed to be empty. There was already someone in there trying to get into the safe. He shot my brother with this."

He lifted up his T-shirt to show a pistol tucked into the belt over his trousers. There was a silencer screwed onto the barrel.

"For fuck's sake, Sanna, are you going tell us what kind of shit you've got us into?"

According to the carabiniere I.D. card in his pocket, the photograph of which matched his unconscious, hook-nose face (minus the bruise on his forehead), he was a captain, Capitano Allegretti. But by now Valentina was almost certain that Allegretti was not his real name and that he was not really a carabiniere, especially given the silencer on his pistol, which one of the Ricciuti brothers was holding. She was not sure whether he was the older or the younger one, because they looked almost like twins to her. She thought of them as the injured one and the other one. The other one was holding the pistol, which was good, because the injured one looked pretty angry, and the only thing keeping him sitting on the bed was his bandaged leg.

Sanna had told the Ricciutis everything, giving them a choice between a massacre or trusting him, and since the brothers were not the murdering type and had left it too late to kill the hook-nosed guy in the office and leave him there, they had chosen the second option. In any case, they lacked the brains to do anything else.

"Uggh!"

Capitano Allegretti, or whatever his name was, began to move, but his eyes stayed shut. He shook his head from side to side, sitting on the floor in a corner, as if to say: "No, give me another five minutes."

"Can we wake him up?" Valentina said.

"But of course," Sanna said, picking up a glass of water from beside the bed and throwing it into Allegretti's face. The captain jumped, breathing in so suddenly that he choked on the water. When he had finished coughing, he looked at Valentina, rubbing his forehead.

"The Bambina," he said in surprise.

"Sorry?"

"It's their nickname for you at the prosecutor's office. Didn't you know?"

There was another one now—a new, less flattering nickname that she would definitely not have liked. His colleagues in the services had spread it around to back up the theory of the jealous trigger-happy boyfriend. But he didn't tell her.

"No, I didn't know."

"What are you doing here? Everyone's looking for you . . ."

He looked around: the little, agitated one, the big guy on the bed with his leg bandaged up, and the other similar-looking one holding the gun. "And who are you? Which department do you work for?"

"I'll ask the questions, if you don't mind. What were you doing in the accountant's secret office?"

"Looking for the accountant."

"No you weren't, you were looking for this."

Valentina patted the red folder lying on the arm of her chair, and saw Allegretti's face twitch for a split second.

"I know what's inside. Transactions, bank account numbers, company names . . . everything I need. What I want to know is who sent you to that office to get these documents. I want to know who you're working for."

"For the state. I'm an officer in the carabinieri."

"Perhaps you were once. Now you're in the secret services."

"That's your interpretation. But even if I was, I'd still be working for the state, wouldn't I?"

"I work for the state as well, but I don't think we're on the same side."

Allegretti smiled. If it wasn't for the hooked nose that made him look like a hawk and coarsened his features, he would have had a nice face.

"They might call you the Bambina, Signorina Lorenzini, but you know how the world works."

"Explain it to me."

"The way it works is that ever since our beloved country has existed, some people have always wanted to change it. Not your average people, perhaps not always the same people, but people with the same interests. And as our wonderful Italian democracy didn't turn out the way they wanted it, they've had to manage the situation. Find other ways to manage our democracy."

"Bombs, files and illegal funds," Sanna said.

Allegretti shrugged. He looked at Valentina, noticing the way she was dressed, in men's clothes that seemed to belong to someone else, then looked again at the others, the little one, the lame one and the other one.

"But who are you?" he asked. "Who the hell—"

"I've already told you that I'm asking the questions."

"Oh really? So we're in your office, are we? This doesn't look the courthouse to me, and these gentlemen don't look like colleagues, and—let's face it, Dottoressa—you don't look like a judge either, dressed like that."

"I asked you who you work for. Answer my question."

Allegretti took off his jacket. He did it slowly, after looking over at the one with the gun as if to ask permission. He shook his head, looking at the lining hanging down from his inside pocket, where they had ripped it to get at his I.D. card, then he folded his jacket on the floor and began to roll up his sleeves.

"What are you doing?" asked the Ricciuti brother with the gun.

"Making myself comfortable," Allegretti said. "I get the feeling this is going to be a long conversation."

"I don't think so," Sanna said. The injured brother got off the bed, landing on his good leg and wobbling slightly before putting the other foot down. Allegretti stopped rolling up his sleeves, looking worried.

"Hey, hey," Valentina said, "what's going on?"

"The judge is stepping out for a moment to smoke a cigarette whilst the officers of the law continue the questioning."

"I don't smoke and I'm not that kind of judge. Some things are off limits."

"Oh, I'm not so sure . . ." Sanna said. "These things happen, don't they?" He looked at the Ricciutis, who nodded. The one with the gunshot wound pushed his hair away from his forehead, revealing a whitish scar.

Allegretti was still too surprised to resist and let them lift him off the floor with no trouble. Valentina sank down into the armchair, pulling up her legs as if to hide behind her knees. She shut her eyes and heard Sanna say "The toilet or the window?" before covering her ears with her hands as well.

Sanna's clothes suited her quite well because he was almost as small and thin as she was. All she had to do was roll up the sleeves of the shirt and the hems of the trousers, which were too big around the waist, but that was fine. The shoes, however, were too small for her, because her feet were one size larger. For a while, Valentina had worn them as best she could, like slip-ons, squashing down the backs under her heel—Sanna didn't have any slippers—but now she had taken them off, and was walking round the garden with the shoes in her hand and the gravel of the path crunching under her bare feet.

She could not stay down there in the basement. The sedative was starting to wear off and she felt wired and restless, as if she had a fever, and her side was hurting. So despite being dizzy and weak, she had ventured up the steps leading to the garden. The air had done her good. Her head was clear and she had started thinking again.

It was not true that she had everything she needed in the red folder. There was probably something there, or perhaps everything, but she was at a loss to understand it. There were transactions, bank accounts and company names, but she was missing the key to interpret them. If she had the accountant, maybe, but who knew where he was. If indeed he really had gone on the run, rather than being killed as well.

Sooner or later she would have to resurface. Go to the carabinieri and turn herself in. Give the folder to the idiot who was running the investigation so he could examine the documents. Yes, but . . . the documents had been illegally obtained, stolen by a bunch of criminals helping her out in secret. Who she could say nothing about because she didn't want them to end up in jail.

Valentina sat down on a step, looking out at the fields beyond the hedge at the bottom of the garden—it really was the countryside over there—and held her head in her hands.

The Bambina, her colleagues called her. The Bambina. When Allegretti had said it, it made her angry, but she had had other things on her mind. Later, it had brought a fleeting smile, but now she wanted to cry, just like a little girl.

What did she think she was doing? She was a judge, and judges didn't run secret investigations. Judges used the police, the carabinieri, the finance police, even the secret services. All the resources offered by the Code of Criminal Procedure. A far cry from her rag-tag bunch of struck-off doctors and housebreakers. Cops and robbers: the cops stay on one side, the robbers on the other.

But what happens when the lines get blurred? Ferro had been killed by people with the same I.D. card as Allegretti.

A shower of objects clattered onto the gravel next to Valentina, and she was hit on the head by something hard, that stung like she had been cut. It was a ten lira coin. She saw it rolling along the step next to a bunch of keys. Then, from above, she heard a hoarse cry, halfway between a growl and a bellow, which made her get up suddenly, ducking her head, before looking up to see Allegretti hanging head first out of the window, his arms spread out in a cross, and the two Ricciuti brothers holding his legs from above.

She went back inside, so shaken that she didn't feel the wound in her side or the burning pain in her scalp. She stopped at the door, stunned, without risking another glance up.

What did she think she was doing? Anything Allegretti said now was of no use to her. In fact, if she so much as mentioned what was happening, she would end up in prison herself. He might have some indication, some clue about the key to interpreting the data, the names of corrupt officials. Something to take to the prosecutor's offices, giving her some sort of justification, so that her investigation wouldn't be ignored. Or perhaps nothing of the sort.

But she had to do one thing immediately. She had to stop this torture. Make them stop, right now.

She walked towards the door, but the sight of a shadow falling down made her pause on the threshold an instant before Allegretti fell past her, hitting the steps with a thud, followed by his belt, broken in two, and a curse from Sanna.

"Once more."

"Again? I've already told you twice."

"Then tell me again. I want to know everything he said."

Sanna sighed.

"O.K. He said there was a war going on and we didn't know what kind of shit we'd got ourselves into."

"Is that how he put it, there's a war going on and you don't know what kind of shit you've got yourself into?"

"No, first the shit and then the war, 'you're in the middle of a war,' to be precise."

"And when was that? While he was hanging upside down?"

"No, when we were in the toilet, between one dip in the pan and the next."

Valentina suppressed a shudder.

"Again, please. And from the beginning."

Sanna heaved another sigh. He had not even been interrogated like this when he was arrested. But after what had happened, he could only do as he was told. The Ricciutis had suggested throwing the judge out of the window as well and making a run for it, but he refused: "Let the Bambina handle it." He had told them in those words—even he called her the Bambina—and the others had nodded in silence. Partly because he had picked up the gun with the silencer and it had not left his hand since.

So he told her for the third time how they had taken Allegretti into the toilet on the ground floor, and the Ricciutis had held his head down in the bowl for almost a minute, but he had said nothing. So back he went for a minute and a half, and had come up spluttering and coughing, but still said nothing. So down for almost two minutes—Sanna had even flushed twice—and when they brought him up he said, "You don't know what kind of shit you've got yourself into." "For now, you're the one who's in the shit," Sanna had replied, and that was when Allegretti had told them "We're in the middle of a war." And since it seemed they had softened him up enough, they had taken him back to the clinic.

That bit Valentina remembered. Allegretti on his knees on the floor, coughing, with a lock of wet hair dangling down over his beak of a nose. Her immobile on the chair, with her arms spread on the armrests like she was sitting in court, trying to looking like an investigating magistrate even though she was wearing Sanna's shirt, his trousers rolled down at the waist and turned up at the ankles, and his moccasins trodden down like espadrilles. At least she was out of the pyjamas.

"You really don't know what's going on out there? You've got no idea what's been stirred up?"

"By my investigations?"

"No, of course not. That's routine. Sometimes a clever little magistrate uncovers one of our deals. And by the way, I've always said that we have to be careful to cover up anything to do with money, more than anything else. Because investigating a murder, the most you're going to find is a murderer. But when you start following a money trail, you never know where it's going to lead."

"Back to the point. What next? You had a routine problem. A clever little magistrate had discovered a company supplying illegal funds."

"Exactly. So you replace the weak link in the chain . . . in this case by smuggling him out of the country because he's still of some use . . . then bump off the magistrate with a plausible excuse and turn the investigation over to one of your own."

At this point, Allegretti had bitten his lip, Valentina remembered clearly. She immediately made a mental note to add "corrupt" to her mental picture of her idiot colleague.

"So what's the problem? That you didn't manage to kill me?"

"No . . . well, yes, that is a problem too, but with all due respect, Dottoressa, that can always be sorted out. No, the problem is that you disappeared. And everyone's wondering who's got you, who took you, who that policeman was working for, because of course no-one believes he just abducted you because he's crazy. So there must be a reason he did it, right? Anyway, you've got me here and I'm not causing any problems, but you must realise that I'm curious. That's practically why I do this job . . . Can you tell me who that policeman was working for? Who these people are? Whose side you're on?"

"In the war?"

"War? What war?"

"That's what you said when we were holding your head down the toilet," Sanna hissed through tight lips, under his bristling moustache. You could see he was getting angrier by the minute.

"Well, you know how it goes, Dottoressa, the people behind the scenes don't always agree amongst themselves. Especially when the old guard don't want to make way for the new guys. That's more or less where we're at now, with some of us sticking with the old lot, and some with the new lot. It's a bad time. You know what happens when everything has to change so that nothing changes."

"No, what happens?"

Allegretti puffed out his cheeks and blew out the air through his half-closed lips. "And not just bombs. Blackmail, files, money and information. And judges."

"Now tell me who's fighting this war. Tell me who they are. Tell me their names."

"It's a long list. You've no idea who's mixed up in this."

"So what are we talking about? A party? A group, a clan, a lodge? What is it?"

Allegretti sighed, saying nothing, and it was clear that from then on, he would do no more than sigh.

"No, no . . . I never said that."

Then Sanna had gestured to the Ricciuti brothers, who grabbed hold of Allegretti's arms, as Valentina sank back down into the armchair, and that was where her recollection ended.

Thinking that holding his head in the toilet bowl would no longer have the same effect, they had taken Allegretti up to the third floor and dangled him upside down out of the window. No-one could see on that side, as the house looked out over the fields. They explained to the captain that he would hit the steps

head first—which was in fact what had happened—and started
to shake him.

The Ricciutis had been holding him, mainly the younger one,
who had grabbed hold of his belt, but the belt had snapped, and
down he had come. Amen.

"Listen," Sanna said, "we're not talking about someone like
Giuseppe Pinelli here, this guy was a real bastard. So there's no
need to get too worked up about him falling out of the window.
Let's just leave him somewhere, end of story."

Valentina did not seem to be listening to him. She had put
her elbow back on the armrest, with her chin in her hand, and
the other hand resting on her good side. Sanna looked at her in
silence. Tight-lipped, with a frown line in the middle of her forehead, between her eyes.

A little girl.

The Bambina.

The judge.

She stayed like that for a while, then turned to Sanna with that
determined look you could not help but obey.

"No," she said.

"No?"

"We're not just going to leave him like that."

"You know we can't call the police . . ."

"Do our friends the brothers know how to steal a car?"

"How do you mean?"

"I don't know, break a window, force the lock. Can they steal
a car?"

"Yes, obviously . . . Yes, they can."

"Then go and steal a car, put Allegretti in the boot and set
fire to it."

Sanna was left open-mouthed, so surprised that he did not
even raise a hand to catch the wallet that Valentina had thrown

to him. It bounced off his chest and fell onto the floor, open at the captain's I.D.

"And make sure this stays intact, somewhere they'll find it."

It all happened in the space of three days.

On the first day, the car containing Allegretti's burned body was discovered. The Ricciutis had left it on the outskirts of Bologna, still close enough to the city that the police and the carabinieri were called, one after the other. As Valentina had expected, a row over who was to blame blew up immediately, highlighting the fact that Allegretti was a carabiniere but not really a carabiniere.

She was sure that the captain's death would further inflame relations between the various secret service departments, and that there must have been coded messages in the newspapers containing reciprocal accusations, peace offers and declarations of war, but she was not in a position to read between the lines and did not try.

The second day, in any case, was all about the press. She sent Sanna on a tour of the shops to photocopy the documents they had stolen from the accountant's office, then sent them to every newspaper that came to mind, along with an anonymous note hinting at the links between a certain company and the secret services, so the press connected the documents to Allegretti's death.

On the third day, the lawyer representing Valentina's boyfriend gave a scathing interview, broadcast on the T.V. news, complaining that his client was being investigated for an attempted crime of passion, whereas it seemed clear that someone had shot Valentina because of her investigations, which seemed to have come dangerously close to rogue fringes of the intelligence services.

That same day, the accountant contacted a journalist from the alternative media from Spain to say he might come back to the country. This was probably one office exerting some sort of pressure on another, but from Valentina's point of view, it helped to make the situation clear-cut enough to decide that the time had come to resurface.

And so on the fourth day, she sent Sanna out to buy her a sweater and a pair of flat shoes, went out to give herself up at the first checkpoint she could find, and came back to life.

She didn't know his name, she had never asked, so when she saw him in the distance with his back to her, all she could do was shout: "Hey!" then "Doctor!"

Sanna turned around. Valentina spread out her arms to signal to the two plainclothes policemen escorting her to stay back, and ran towards him, as he thought: "Shit, she really does look like a girl." She was not wearing the sweater, because they were a couple of days into August and the heat was fierce, but she had also had her hair cut, making her look like a teenager.

"See," she said, "I kept my promise. I'm not a traitor."

She had told the police that she had been sedated right up until she managed to escape, from whereabouts and captors unknown. She had revealed nothing of use, and no-one had held her head in the toilet bowl to get any more out of her.

"But don't expect any special treatment if we meet again. Professionally, I mean."

"I can't see you coming back again to get yourself patched up in my surgery."

"I meant in my professional capacity."

"I know."

Strange how they both felt they had so much to say but were embarrassed to put it into words.

It had happened to Sanna before, when he had held hands with armed robbers as if they were little boys, and to Valentina, when she had spent evenings or nights poring over papers in the office with colleagues from the police or the carabinieri. When it was all over, they went back to being strangers.

"I'd like to know your name," Valentina said.

"I'd rather you didn't," Sanna replied. "How's your investigation going? I've been seeing your name in the papers."

And the nickname too, every so often: the Bambina.

"It's stalled. I know—it hasn't even been a month yet, and there's still so much to check, but I know when something's ground to a halt."

She'd brought the accountant back to Italy, arrested a few white-collar types, and a couple of secret service colonels had resigned. Her corrupt, idiot colleague had been charged and suspended. She'd uncovered a nice racket generating illegal funds, but no more than that. No-one had ever mentioned anything bigger—no party, clan or lodge, old or new—let alone come up with a list of important names.

"At least we got some payback for Ferro," Sanna said.

Valentina motioned again for the policemen to stay back.

"I think we did more than that. We showed them that they can't just do what they want, go over our heads and behind our backs, as if we were puppets you can just get rid of."

"And you think that they'll stop killing people and planting bombs to help them . . . what did that guy say? 'Manage our democracy'?"

"I don't know, but every time there's an investigation like this one, however far it gets, we're putting a spanner in the works, and sooner or later the machine will stop."

"Do you really believe that?"

"I do. I've figured it out now. Otherwise I wouldn't do this job."

Sanna's lips twitched underneath his moustache. By then, Valentina had learnt to tell a smile from a grimace, and now he was smiling.

"Marco Sanna," he said, holding out his hand.

Just then, a deafening roar rang out through the still August air, followed by a rumble that kept reverberating round the sky like an endless roll of thunder.

Many of the people under the arcades had fallen to the ground in shock, and Sanna and Valentina had also dropped to their knees on the pavement, holding hands, heads hunched down into their shoulders.

When they got up and walked out from under the arcade, into the street, they saw a column of thick black smoke rising from the direction of the station.

Translated by Alan Thawley

Giancarlo De Cataldo

THE TRIPLE DREAM OF THE PROSECUTOR

The ease with which the West has capitulated to organized crime makes me think that there is an indestructible bond between the Mafia and democracy. Thanks to the flow of capital that organized crime pours day after day into various strategic sectors of the economy, our democracy is able to survive and flourish, even in the face of recurrent financial crises.

The accumulation of the ill-gotten gains of the Mafia needs to be rationalized within a complex legislative and judicial system. On the one hand it is essential that they continue to deceive the general population that society is governed by politics and the law, and on the other to ensure, in the course of two or at most three generations, the complete integration of organized crime. Today, Mafiosi are the new soldiers of fortune; they guarantee the system stays on track and they will usher in a new dawn. Their children and grandchildren will form a new elite destined to inherit the West.

—Theolonious Lecinsky, "Democracy and Conspiracy"
Samanthowanatan University Press, 2010

PROLOGUE

Novere, Italy, 1966.

"ATTENTION PLEASE, CHILDREN, A MOMENT OF YOUR ATTEN-
tion! Today I'm going to teach you a new game. Listen up!"

So said the new teacher at the The Bandiera Brothers Elementary School, in the little town of Novere, speaking to his
class on 1 October, 1966. He was a lively young man with wire-
rimmed glasses, a woolly jumper and corduroy trousers. He had
taken the place of the old teacher, an ex-official of Mussolini's
Italian Social Republic, who had been known for his casual use
of the cane—and for his strange habit of ending the Lord's Prayer
each day by saying "so it is."

"Little idiots, what is this 'so it may be'? How dare you doubt
the word of He Who Is All Powerful? You must say, 'So it is,' for
heaven's sake!"

And down would come the cane on the naughty ones, a punishment he meted out with great vigour, before returning quickly
to his chair and opening the register with one hand, while strok-
ing his moustache with the other. But the new teacher, Vito,

never raised his voice, nor handed out blows left and right, and apart from his utter inability to master the correct pronunciation of "e" and "o"—a legacy of his origins in Puglia—he seemed to be a strong, likeable sort. Above all, he knew how to enthuse the students: he really involved them, asking them their opinions about everything and making them feel important, and yes, almost (but only "almost," mind you) like adults.

"O.K., the game is this, boys. We all live in a democracy. Do you know what that is? Have your parents explained it to you? Anyone like to answer? Right, go ahead, Ottavio."

"Democracy is our form of government. It means that we're all equal and we have a duty to vote in elections."

"Nearly right. Well done! Anyone else? Pierfiliberto!"

"Democracy means that everyone wants to eat but nobody wants to work."

"Hmm . . . interesting. Did you come up with that concept yourself, Pierfiliberto?"

"My father says so. And he also says that things were better when they were worse."

"I see . . . Well, now I'll explain the game that we're going to play tomorrow."

He began with some background. Beginning with Pericles, the great leader who gave equality to the citizens of Athens, he went on to tell the story of Brutus and Cassius and their vain attempt to liberate Rome from tyranny, then spoke of the English barons and their Magna Carta, which limited the powers of the king. Coming to Italy, he talked about Machiavelli and the Medici, who ruled a free and flourishing Florence, and on to the French Revolution and the Rights of Man.

He paused for a moment and then, slowly scanning their faces, he began to tell them about the wars that their forefathers had fought to create a free and united Italy. He spoke of this and much more, for quite some time, this Vito, and his students were rapt. Who knows if they understood it all; for example, when he began to speak about the Bandiera brothers, who gave their name to the school; according to the teacher they were young and noble heroes of Italian unification—in truth, this was a bit of a surprise. The students in Class 5C had only ever seen them as two ugly statues—plaster busts, covered in spit, cigarette butts stubbed out in their empty eye sockets, decorated all over with obscene slogans.

But even if they didn't understand everything, one thing that was certainly clear was that from now on, they could elect their own head boy for the year. This was a radical move—their old teacher had always chosen the head boy himself. And each year, without fail, he had chosen Pierfiliberto Berazzi-Perdicò. This was because he was the tallest, the broadest, the roughest, and naturally, the biggest telltale. In a word, the nastiest. Perfect, therefore, in the eyes of the old teacher, who saw it as his mission to maintain order through force. One of the jobs he gave his teacher's pet was to put at least six or seven names per day up on the blackboard in the column marked "bad boys," who would then be caned. As for the good, putting up one name a week, his own, was more than sufficient.

A tremor of joy and excitement rippled through the students when they realised there was revolution in the air. And to the few obstinate ones who insisted that this would change nothing, young Ottavio explained that, in fact, the opposite was true: everything would change. No more arbitrary punishments, no more bullying or harassment or caning, nor more head-boy-as-pawn of a brutal teacher. At last, democracy had arrived.

"So let's all vote for you!" Donato Casati shouted out straight away. Donato was the runt of the class—a little blonde weakling, and thus one of Pierfiliberto's preferred victims. He loved to get his kicks calling the kid all sorts of rude names—including his personal favourites: Girlie, Bedwetter and Four-Eyes.

"Me or any one of us, it's all the same to me," Ottavio shrugged, "as long as it's not him!"

"It has to be you!"

Standing before the group, feeling the staunch support of his twenty-four heroic comrades-in-arms, Ottavio experienced the first thrill of vanity in his young life.

Pierfiliberto had also scented the wind of change. Those miserable bedwetting girlie four-eyed bastards had all ganged up against him—and now he would lose power. No-one would ever be afraid of him again. Never again would they do his homework, in fear of his retaliation if they refused. Goodbye, the coveted striker's shirt in matches at the weekend; now they would all shout out loud what was already known but nobody had ever dared say openly before—that Pierfiliberto was totally hopeless at football. A catastrophe was looming . . .

And the great enemy, Ottavio, standing against him, was the only one who had never been afraid of him in the past—the only one who had stoically rolled with the punches he gave him with that unbearable little prattish smile of his; now that very prat Ottavio would triumph.

It couldn't happen. It must not happen.

And lo and behold . . . it didn't.

Those little shits had "reckoned without the innkeeper." Pierfiliberto had no idea what the hell that expression actually meant; his father used to say it on occasion, at the height of the odd major domestic dispute. It was the killer line that reduced his mother to silence and restored harmony in the family. If it worked at home, it would work in school; Pierfiliberto wasn't the type to surrender without a fight.

There were twenty-four hours left before the election. The teacher had made a grave error. He had given the opposition time to organise. If they had voted immediately, carried on a wave of emotion after that lecture about the great Pericles and all those other old farts, Pierfiliberto's destiny would have been sealed. But Master Vito had made a mistake . . .

An idea was needed; it came in the night. On the morning of the elections Ottavio immediately sensed that something was up. Donato Casati, who the day before had been his biggest supporter, slunk past him, eyes downcast, as he went to drop his ballot in the urn which had been placed next to the teacher's desk. Pierfiliberto had voted with ostentatious confidence, flanked by three or four of those who, the day before, had pledged their eternal fidelity to Ottavio. When the teacher announced the result, a guilty silence descended on class 5C.

"Berazzo-Perdicò, twenty-five votes. Mandati, one vote. I declare Pierfiliberto Berazzi-Perdicò the head boy until the end of the school year."

Ottavio's eyes misted over. He had to fight with all his might to hold back the flood of angry tears that threatened to erupt. No way. He would never cry in front of Pierfiliberto, never! No-one noticed that he was making a huge effort not to bawl his head off; he just smiled a strained smile as, one by one, the renegades dutifully gave him friendly pats on the back. No-one noticed that the winner was giving him a hostile smirk either, nor the slightly bitter tone with which Master Vito had announced the result. "My compliments," he told the class. "Today you have had a fine test run of democracy."

That same day, as they were leaving, Donato Casati revealed the scam to Ottavio. To tell the truth, Ottavio didn't really want to hear it, and when the others approached, he did everything to avoid them. But, in the end, curiosity won out over anger. How did it go? Simple. Pierfiliberto bought the votes. One by one. The price: collector's edition comics, and no holding back on the good ones: *Tex*, still in its striped packaging, *Capitan Miki* and *Black Macigno*, and the brightly illustrated *Intrepido*. There was also chewing gum, new notebooks and rare Panini-brand stickers that you could re-use again and again.

Once Donato Casati left, Vito, who had also heard all of this, came up to Ottavio and gave him a paternal hug. "This was a hard lesson, but it will serve you well. You are as strong as a lion cub, you'll bounce back."

And the story is not finished yet. A few days later, a contrite Donato Casati sidled up to Ottavio during break.

"Pierfiliberto has taken back everything he gave us. The comics, the stickers, everything! He also said that from tomorrow we all have to take it in turns to buy him a snack. He said now that he's been elected we have to give back all his stuff!"

"What am I meant to do about that?"

"You have to tell the teacher! Then he'll annul the election and call a new vote."

"Ah. No, I don't think so," Ottavio said. "You chose him and you have to keep him."

And even as he spoke, he was suffused with a marvellous sensation of defeat. He couldn't know it yet, little Ottavio, but it was exactly that self-serving self-pity that Teresa would go on to reproach him for all his life. 'Gadzooks!'—to quote the beloved Black Macigno—he was far too much like the Roman leader Cincinnatus, who conceded power as soon as the war was over, and he was proud of it.

Pierfiliberto remained as the head boy for the whole year. But since their teacher Vito was very different from the old teacher, it was soon clear that his role was only a formality. Incapable of fully grasping this, the first time Vito had to go off for a meeting with the headmaster, Pierfiliberto rushed up to the blackboard, drew a line down the middle and chalked in "good boys" on the left and "bad boys" on the right and began to scribble a load of names in the second column. He got up to fifteen (with Ottavio at the top of the list) when the teacher returned suddenly.

"What do you think you're doing, Pierfiliberto?"

"The good boys and the bad, sir!"

"And where did you get this brilliant idea?"

"I always did this with our old teacher. And then he doled out punishment to the bad boys."

"Punishment?"

"Ten strokes with the cane, sir!"

"Maybe you don't get it, my boy. I'm not your old teacher. There is no caning here, or anything of that kind. Now get back to your seat! If you ever try this nonsense again, I'll revoke your role as head boy."

"You can't do that, sir. I was elected by my fellows. This is a democracy."

The teacher looked at his students. They were all falling about laughing, enjoying Pierfiliberto's joke, his quick wit. Vito felt sorry for them and for himself. Only Ottavio didn't join in the laughter, and looked quite disgusted. Vito felt sorry for him too—and for a split second he thought that democracy might just be a bad idea.

1

Novere, Italy, Present Day

ONE NIGHT, OTTAVIO MANDATI, PROSECUTOR FOR THE ITALian Republic at the court of Novere, had a dream. Two men dressed in black knocked on his door and told him they had a court order to arrest him. These guys were in every way identical to Bardolfo and Pistola, the two old coppers that had worked with him forever. Had it not been a dream, the prosecutor would have laughed his head off. Bardolfo and Pistola were well-known jokers, hard-core Tuscans, who would rather poke out their eyes than give up a good prank. To present a senior magistrate with an order for his arrest—with his own signature on it! Ah, this practical joke was a real beauty.

But it was a dream. And Mandati knew from the start that he was dreaming. He loved to dream. So he only took a quick look at the document they gave him, without really dwelling on the signature.

"Papa! What's happening?"

Lucio was his only son, a big awkward lad of twenty-two, who was reluctantly studying law and adored rock music. He chased after unattainable girls, and was in turn chased by other more available girls, whom he regularly turned down—as his father learned from the odd clandestine foray onto his Facebook. When Teresa caught him sneaking a peek, he defended himself weakly: "I'm doing it for you too—it isn't right that our son cuts us out of his world!" She gave him a withering look.

"Well, Papa, what's up?"

That morning, like many others, his son was just returning home. From a concert, from a lover, from who knows where. He mustn't find out the truth—even if it was only a dream, he must not. The prosecutor shot a look at his two guardian angels and they nodded in complicity.

"Nothing, really . . . something's come up at work . . . now get to bed, you—what bags you have under your eyes!"

Relieved, the prosecutor who arrested himself climbed in the back seat of the armoured car, an old Alfetta, shivering a little in his light kimono decorated with a design of the snow-covered Mount Fujiyama, which he had thrown on in a hurry over his striped pyjamas. Pistola got behind the wheel, Bardolfo next to him. The old Alfetta didn't start smoothly—there was a sinister sound, a rattling of metal. For six months, from the point when the government subsidy had stopped, it was Mandati who had paid for the petrol, from his own pocket.

As for the kimono and the pyjamas, they were gifts from Teresa. The kimono was a souvenir of a post-adolescent trip to the Land of the Rising Sun. The pyjamas were a souvenir of a rather more prosaic trip to an outlet shop near Lake Lugano. Two garments which were by now old and tatty, not at all presentable in public. Still, Mandati had a soft spot for them—they reminded him of the spiky affection of his life's companion, and the tender moments they had shared. And also, naturally, of the irritated flash in her eyes that was always there during their endless discussions. Anyway, who would ever appear in company, if that is what you would call it, in kimono and pyjamas, if not the protagonist of a dream?

They were cruising along, surrounded by a strange luminous yellow light that may have come from the dim rows of street-lights, or from the dirty windows of the huge silhouetted housing blocks, as they passed through the "Pep Zone." This housing estate was the masterpiece of the mayor—his biggest scam ever, the mother of all his malfeasance. He had granted 327 building permits in one night to modify the official plan for the area, for the benefit of fifteen companies with very catchy names: Flowering Field, Dawn Light, The Marvelous Fountainhead, Blue Horizon. The owners? All frontmen for the mayor.

In one morning, the bulldozers had rolled in and destroyed the old elementary school, the historic garden with the benches and the memorial dedicated to The Fallen of Novere "in all the wars for the defence of the country." Not a single one of the forty-eight tall, shady plane trees was saved.

At the time, Mandati, who was a young assistant prosecutor, started asking questions and initiated an investigation. The head prosecutor, Smilzi-Trionfi, immediately called him in for a meeting. "The people of Novere are asking for houses for themselves and for their children, Mandati. Do you want to explain to me what the hell all this has got to do with us, or the law? Eh? You want search warrants? Arrests? Don't even think about it!" And he closed the case, which died an instant and painless death in the archives. But this was all in the past, as Teresa would remind him now and then.

"You get a sick pleasure from reliving your defeats, Ottavio. Sulking and self-pity don't produce anything but bile."

They were now passing by the prison, without stopping. Mandati began to question his guardian angels, but they just shrugged. Maybe they were going to skip the prison and go straight in front of the judge? Even so, they ought to register the arrest. This dream doesn't have the correct procedure, the prosecutor noted, with faint irony.

In front of the court, a little crowd was waiting in the dim light of dawn. Early swallows circled in the sky, heralding a sunny day ahead. Mandati made out some familiar faces in the crowd: murderers, thieves and rapists whom he had tried, but sometimes failed, to send down. They waited there, quiet and composed, while he got out of the Alfetta. He saw they were mingling with some other notable faces: the victims of crimes for whom he had sought, but not always obtained, justice.

He recognised the widow Schirinzi. Her husband, a young casual worker, had been killed due to the negligent management of a building site, which lacked even the most basic health and safety regulations. And over there was little Teodori, slumped in a wheelchair. He was only thirteen when the son of one of Novere's leading families ran him over during a drag race with no headlights, one early winter's morning, after a big night out fuelled with booze, girls and cocaine. In court this crime got turned around on the little lad: what was he thinking, crossing the street in front of a decent chap who was just minding his own business? "What? He was afraid of missing the school bus? Tough! He could have got up earlier!"

Bardolfo and Pistola flanked the prosecutor on either side. The little crowd waited as they started to go up the steps, then followed behind them in an orderly fashion. Mandati turned around. In vain he tried to decipher their expressions, searching for resentment, disappointment, even revenge. Nothing. Their stony faces didn't express more than a shared, icy indifference.

Suddenly, from those inscrutable figures arose a sinister murmur. Mandati struggled to understand the meaning of this noise—and how could they make it, when all their mouths were closed? What the devil were they trying to say to him? "Ab . . . aband . . ." Ah, he got it: "Abandon all hope ye who enter here."

For the first time since the beginning of the dream, Mandati felt fear. And this fear turned to terror when, seated on the bench, he glimpsed the unmistakable profile of Pierfiliberto Berazzi-Perdicò, Mayor of Novere. He was wearing the black robes, tied with a gold belt, of an Inquisitor. The prosecutor who had arrested himself was to be accused by the accused . . .

2

Escorted by the faithful Bardolfo and Pistola, Mandati arrived outside the court at 9:00 a.m. on the dot on March 18. It was a rainy Monday, with a cold, wet wind blowing. A filthy day. The climate in those parts had never been up to much. Pierfiliberto Berazzi-Perdicò had made it even worse by knocking down the larch wood that for many long years had eased both the harsh winters and the stormy, muggy summers.

To be fair, the building of The Golden Hill development in its place had given a big boost to the local economy and it had captured, with its undeniable charms, high-end tourism that Novere needed and deserved. So who cares about a handful of scrubby old trees?

"Now, Dottor Mandati, aren't you tired already of persecuting our mayor?"

Tafano Tafàni, the star journalist of T.V. Novere, with a tattooed assistant and one of those ice-cream cone microphones in his hand, pounced on him at the foot of the steps. Five or six junior reporters, equipped with digital recorders, kept a more respectful distance, ready to catch a few sound bites. Over the years, Mandati had learned to stick to a few basic rules. One: never speak to a hostile journalist. Two: Never lose your cool. So he gave the guy, who loved to think of himself as The Voice of Free Novere a big, reassuring smile and tried to scoot past him. But Tafàni was hard on his heels.

"Oh, don't you speak to the free press, Prosecutor? How come? Do you know that according to the latest poll Mayor Berazzi-Perdicò has the support of 75 per cent of our citizens? Results which—"

Restraining his men with a peremptory nod (they would have happily thumped him, reviving the memory of their glorious boxing days at the old gym back home in Rosignano Marittima), Mandati carried on up the fourteen mottled marble steps, crossing the threshold into the court.

With Mandati leading the pack and striving to ignore Tafàni, who in turn was striving to make him listen, while Bardolfo and Pistola were striving not to beat him up, and the junior reporters striving to be more senior reporters . . . no question about it, it was quite a scene. Passers-by stopped to watch, some with a smile, some with a wave—although the young lawyers turned away, averting their eyes, with the clear intention of making their disapproval of the prosecutor's case very plain.

Before reaching the anteroom for the preliminary hearing, Mandati stopped in front of a mirror. His tie knot looked straight. His outfit, dignified and modest, never over the top, and—bless him—without any concession to eccentricity, gave him that ultra-respectable but rather prattish look that people expect from a prosecutor. When he tried to explain to Lucio why he dressed like this, his son laughed sarcastically.

"But Papa, you don't dress like that to be noticed, or because people ask you to. It's because you *are* respectable—and a bit of prat."

The judge for the preliminary hearing, a chubby, jovial colleague of his, was late. Tafano Tafàni grabbed the chance to record a recap for the T.V. special report on the trial, which would be on air in a continuous loop all afternoon.

3

OF FIFTEEN LEGAL ACTIONS BROUGHT AGAINST BERAZZI-Perdicò over the years, only four ended in his acquittal, with a ruling that had established his "innocence." In five cases, requests for indictment had been disregarded, and six times the indictment won by Mandati had been superseded by changes to the law which had been enacted while the trial was ongoing.

His colleague was late. Even the illustrious defendant's dodgy legal entourage hadn't made an appearance yet. Mandati asked Bardolfo and Pistola to let him know when everything was ready to go, and went outside to smoke a good Tuscan cigar on the little paved terrace, which was covered in chewing gum and pigeon droppings. Naturally, the cleaning contract at the court had been given, by private arrangement, to a firm owned by a city counsellor connected to the mayor. Another pillar of the Novere community.

The first puffs of the cigar left him breathless—damn, he was getting old. Even in this respect Berazzi-Perdicò was miles apart from him. They were the same age, but the mayor seemed like his little brother. He didn't smoke, didn't drink, and went jogging for two hours every day. They said he slept little, yet he was possessed of an animal energy, like a cross between a ram and an alien. It was no wonder that so many loved him. Were it not for some minor details—like his criminal character, the fact that he was a pathological liar and an instinctive predator, why, even Mandati would have found him likeable!

On a scaffold on the other side of the courtyard, two workers hammered feebly on a wobbly sheet of metal. Even the court had its story. And how could it be otherwise, in Novere? It was built in the mid '80s, on a plot of land owned by Rocco and Saro Pantaleo, two brothers from Plati who passed away in the subsequent years due to acute lead poisoning.

Between the land acquisition, the licensing and construction, the procurement and rebuilding (at one point a serious asbestos problem was also discovered), the mayor received a small fortune in bribes. And he came out of the subsequent enquiries as clean as a newborn baby out of a bath. Every time Ottavio set foot in the court, he had to find the strength not to vomit; he was sitting in the product of the mayor's dirty deals, and administering justice in his name.

Bardolfo and Pistola, breathless, broke into the flow of his memories.

"Dottor, come, hurry, there's a crisis!"

4

AT 8:45, AS HE PREPARED TO GET INTO HIS BLACK LEXUS RX 450 parked in the large driveway of his family home, the mayor, Pierfiliberto Barazzi-Perdicò, was joined by his son Terenzio. His lawyer, Appella, who was stuck in a traffic jam on the ring road, was calling him urgently. But the call had come on his landline.

"Why didn't he call me on my mobile?"

The boy responded by holding up his mobile, which he had left behind in the toilet. The mayor followed the boy inside. He just had time to hold the phone to his ear when a violent explosion pierced the air.

Bardolfo and Pistola briefed Mandati during the trip to the Villa Maria hospital: apparently the Lexus was thrown high in the air—it was probably a remote-controlled explosive device. The shock waves shattered all the glass within a hundred metres, and a pair of trees fell down.

"The driver?"

"The mayor doesn't have a driver. He loves to drive himself in his 100,000 Euro S.U.V."

"Typical. O.K., so no-one was killed . . ."

"Or injured. The mayor's been admitted to hospital as a pre-caution, suffering from shock."

"Maybe he did it himself, to delay the trial," Bardolfo said under his breath.

The prosecutor shook his head.

"No, that's not his way. How much did you say that S.U.V. was worth?"

"100,000 Euros."

"And does it seem to you that Don Pierfiliberto is the type to sacrifice such an expensive vehicle when, if he wanted to get a postponement, all he needed was a medical certificate? No, it wasn't him."

"Maybe he was just leasing the car! Or it's an insurance scam?"

"It's a possibility. But for the moment . . . for the moment, there's an attempted murder and a victim: Pierfiliberto. Let's see if maybe, for once, we're on the same side."

In the clinic, a pair of overwrought nursing sisters directed them to a small private waiting room. Villa Maria was one of four private clinics in Novere—the most prestigious and efficient.

Ah, the business of the clinics. Another issue Mandati had with the mayor—he sure had been slapped around by that man. Once upon a time, Novere had one public hospital, which functioned perfectly well. At a certain point, a flood of complaints had begun—against the doctors, the management and the nurses: all claims of medical negligence. Members of the local council championed furious, tearful relatives. The victims of these claims went from the granny in her nineties with advanced Parkinson's, to the alcoholic with liver failure from drinking his own homebrew. Every blessed demise inevitably ended up in a file on the prosecutor's desk. And he, inevitably, set them aside, earning him the label of "the hated defender of poor healthcare."

What was he meant to do? The claims were blatantly specious, to the point of absurdity. What the hell was going on with his fellow citizens? Now they were taking issue with Mother Nature? Didn't they realise that every human being is born and then, inexorably, dies?

The mystery was solved when, three months after the claims tsunami, the region was given notice of a new Health Plan. The Novere hospital was one of three that were downgraded from a general hospital to an emergency department only. In practice, for all health issues greater than an ingrown toenail, the people of Novere had to go to the hospital of Vaglio di Sotto, eighty kilometres away, or the one in the regional capital, 150 kilometres away. Or . . . they could pop into one of the four private clinics that Mayor Pierfiliberto Berazzi-Perdicò controlled, either directly or through an intermediary.

And while the restructuring and closing of hospitals was met with indignant reactions throughout the region, ranging from someone spitting in the face of the assessor to a big demonstration blocking a street (with a student in Minisola Castromontana threatening to set himself on fire like a Tibetan monk), in Novere, and only in Novere, the citizens approved the decision.

Mandati went in with all guns blazing to that enquiry. He indicted Berazzi-Perdicò and the entire city council. But the trial was stillborn—the proceedings were formally adjourned. The fall guys were two drunken octogenarians, who testified that they had won the lottery and, thanks to this, had decided all of a sudden, and very shrewdly, to invest in the health sector and fund the clinics. Mandati's claims against the mayor and his cronies were dropped, one after another.

T.V. Novere raised the stakes, making much of the fact that Mandati was defending the "public hospital of a hundred deaths" because it was the only one in the area that gave work to abortion doctors. They said he was the enemy of life and a champion of the moral decay of society. Joining the chorus were a bishop, several nuns (who were in charge of the four clinics) and a couple of undersecretaries.

Mandati was tried at the high council of the magistrate's court. Berazzi-Perdicò's pithy comment on his eventual acquittal was a memorable phrase, reported by the faithful Tafano Tafàni: "Dog don't eat dog." Even years later, if Mandati or his wife or son needed any tests done, they went the eighty kilometres to the hospital in Vaglio di Sotto rather than setting foot in enemy territory.

And now, the head doctor sent word that his illustrious patient was ready to receive them.

"But don't put him under any stress, eh? He's had a tough time."

"Who? That one? Come on . . ." Pistola said.

Silencing him with a sharp look, Mandati went ahead of the doctor, making his way into the Berazzi-Perdicò Ward (in case anyone were to forget who was in charge in Novere). Pierfiliberto was sprawled in a big, plush armchair. He was in a suit and tie with his pink cheeks perfectly shaved, and his face fixed in that winsome smile of an eternal teenager which his constituents found so irresistible.

"Hello, Signor Mayor."

"Why don't you relax, Otta? Can't you see that this time we're on the same side? I am the victim. And you have to find out who the evil bastards are that want to kill me."

Then he launched into a little speech, an endless variation of his favourite theme since the dawn of their acquaintance: "Why can't we be friends, Ottavio?"

5

THE FIRST TIME THAT PIERFILIBERTO HELD OUT HIS HAND IN friendship was at the end of the school year in 1967.

"O.K., I played a joke on you with that whole head boy thing, but at the end of the day, it wasn't worth it. Anyway, it was only a bit of fun. What do you say we become friends, you and I?"

Other offers rained down in the successive years: in middle school, he came with a proposal to work together on a recycled pastry scheme.

"I'll meet you at 7:30 a.m. at Franco's Bar and we'll buy all the sixty lire pastries. Then we'll bring them to school and resell them for seventy. I reckon that in the whole of the Mazzini School there are five grades with five classes in each one, so that's twenty-five classes, and if you say on average there are twenty-five students per class, that means we can sell 625 pastries. Netting ten lire per piece, we can make 6,250 lire a day! Even if you allow for absences, for students who are off sick, or those with irritating parents who prepare them a lunchbox at home, we can still say we'll probably net 5,000 lire a day. That's 2,500 each! What do you say? Not bad, eh? Just think of all the great stuff you can buy for 2,500 lire a day! Which adds up to 50,000 lire a month! Not exactly peanuts—do you know how much a school caretaker earns in a month, Otta?"

Predictably, Ottavio told him to go to hell.

The recycling of the pastries, with some more sophisticated variations (for example on Mondays they sold the leftovers from Sunday that they got from the *Torquato* pastry shop, in the neighbouring village of Sant'Anselmo) was, in the end, organised with the help of the school caretaker, Santissimi, known as "Jaws" because he was so greedy.

When they got to Pisacane, their high school—where attendance was compulsory for local middle-class children like Pierfiliberto and Ottavio—the second proposal was mooted:

"You know Teodorico, the supply teacher for Latin and Greek? The one with the long beard who smells of fish and thinks he's a poet? A poet—go figure! For sure, this loser Teodorico would be on the street if he didn't have good connections with the school board. I think he's shagging Signorina Montegazza, the history teacher with the huge tits . . . anyway, he would sell his own mother for money. So hear me out: he's in a position to know the content of the translation essay they're giving us in the morning. He'll know the afternoon beforehand, you follow me? So here's what I thought: Teodorico can do the translation. I think we'll get it for 5,000, at the most 6,000, or maybe 6,500 because he's always desperate.

"Then we'll make photocopies for our fellow students, including those who are on the borderline of failing but might just make it, and those who are total lost causes but still have hope. Follow me? Good. At the absolute minimum, we'll sell around twenty copies each time we have a go. We'll sell them for 7,000 to the ones whose grades are hanging in the balance, and 10,000 to the condemned. They're morons, but if they want to save themselves they have to risk something, don't you think? So let's say, on an average of 8,000 lire, we make 160,000 each time; so subtracting the five or six thousand for our supplier, or even allowing ten thousand for him—being very generous, because he's such a loser—there's still a profit of 150,000. That's 75,000 for each of us. Understand, Otta? He takes ten, and we take 75,000 each. Just desserts for taking chances!

"Now, there are three essays per term in Latin and three in Greek, which makes six. 150 multiplied by six is 900. At the end of the year we'll have about 500,000 lire profit. Oh and hang about—this is a bombshell: Teodorico is also trying to get hold of the maths tests, although mark my words, he won't hand those over for less than 20,000 each . . ."

"And why not the Italian essays as well?" Ottavio ventured, fighting between disgust and a desire to see how far Pierfilberto would go. What were his limits, if any?

"Are you stupid? Oh, don't make me regret speaking to you about this. Those essays, they're personal. They're all about what we think of the world. It's impossible to copy them—they'd suss it straight away!"

In that precise moment, Ottavio understood that Pierfilberto wasn't just greedy, petty and quite brazenly indifferent to the rules. He was also smart, this boy. Smart, and as he would demonstrate in the years to come, sometimes unpredictable and inspired.

"Sorry, but why don't you just do this alone, this fine scheme of yours? What do you need me for?"

"My dear Ottavio. I'm one of those kids who are barely passing at school, while you are at the top of the class in every subject. Suppose they caught us—it won't happen, but let's just suppose they did, why, you could say that you did it for humanitarian reasons, to protest against the system, you know? You're a leftie, aren't you? You can invent something! That's it. Protesting against the system. They couldn't do anything to you. In fact, you'd be a hero. Come on, say yes!"

Ottavio said no.

But some years later, they did genuinely come close to becoming friends. It was around 1980, more or less. Mandati was studying hard to pass the exam for the magistrature. He'd lost track of Berazzi-Perdicò over the years—different universities, different paths and ambitions. One fine day, Berazzi-Perdicò returned to Novere with big projects in mind.

"Now see here, my friend. You've asked why, despite your obvious reluctance, I have constantly tried to make friends with you for all these years. Now I'll explain. I learned—no, I understood immediately, from as early as I can remember—that men divide into two categories: the idiots and the supermen. The idiots are the masses: it's easy to control them, just give them what they want. Or rather, what I want. I have clear ideas in regard to this . . . very clear ideas. But the supermen, *we* supermen, if you'll allow me to say so, because I hold you in the greatest esteem and respect and I consider you a superman, like me . . . and in this respect we're very similar, more than friends—we're brothers, Ottavio, brothers, eh? Sorry. Where were we?"

"We supermen . . ."

"Ah, yes, we supermen, we don't have to be at war with each other. We need to be on the same side. Nature demands it. Our energies should not be wasted in a fratricidal war—we need to cooperate for the progress of humanity!"

"Excuse me, don't you think you're exaggerating a little? The progress of humanity?"

"Only the idiots set limits. We supermen have a duty to think big."

Every time he cast his mind back to that period, Mandati felt a mixture of embarrassment, shame and rage. The fact was that Berazzi-Perdicò seemed to have changed, after all those years. Gone were the rough edges and aggression of adolescence. He'd been able to transform his native greed into a sort of messianic force. He'd become taller and slimmer. He knew how to fit in with people now, and they adored him. He had a fiancée with a prestigious name—a sort of countess with vast property holdings—and declared himself ready to risk everything he had to wake up the sleepy town of Novere.

He made continuous references to the change he could bring, badgering Mandati, who sensed behind the words a great if unscrupulous energy. Maybe it really was possible to do it all. Around the same time, many of Mandati's old certainties were wavering. The political faith, that naive political faith that he had held dear through his university years had been sunk in a storm of disillusion fuelled by all the pointless terrorist violence. And Teresa was obstinately resisting his courtship . . . in short, everything was going wrong for him; he was on his knees. So he started hanging out with Berazzi-Perdicò, who had launched himself into the world of property speculation and was starting to show a definite interest in politics . . .

A discreet cough from Bardolfo and Pistola brought him back to reality, and he tried to focus on what was happening.

The two cops were staring at him, confusion in their faces. Berazzi-Perdicò, sprawled in the armchair, gazed at him with furrowed brow. "You don't suffer from narcolepsy, do you, Otta? You've not been with us for the last ten minutes! If you do have this problem, I know the top specialists . . ."

"Tell me exactly what happened, please," Mandati said through gritted teeth, regaining his composure. It cost him a great effort to take a neutral and professional tone.

6

THREE DAYS AFTER THE ATTEMPT ON THE MAYOR'S LIFE, while Bardolfo, Pistola, sixteen other carabinieri, twenty-four policemen and two secret service agents raked over every possible lead in the case, Pierfiliberto Berazzi-Perdicò, sitting at his desk in his office, sifting through the letters of solidarity and comfort that had poured in from high and low, decided he wanted a pastry: a *cannolo*. His faithful secretary, a woman of unimpeachable values who was certifiably ugly (as the mayor always said, beautiful women don't need to work; if they did, what would the ugly ones do?) took just twenty minutes to appear with a tray of these Sicilian sweets, bought from the excellent *Turiddu* pastry shop on the Corso Vittorio Emanuele III.

It was a sunny day—the windows were thrown open wide. Berazzi-Perdicò, salivating over the delicious dense mass of ricotta scattered with chocolate chips, tore open the wrapping. At that moment, a hungry pigeon, which must been lurking nearby for a while, catapulted down onto the desk and stuck his beak in a *cannolo*.

Caught by surprise, the mayor was unable to contain a surge of revulsion; he grabbed a paperweight and threw it at the bird, but missed the target. The pigeon, not a bit frightened, pecked out a nice piece of flaky pastry and began to eat it. Berazzi-Perdicò called for help—the secretary came running. The pigeon broke away from the tray and looked around in frantic dismay, then made a strange noise, halfway between a gulp and a burp, turned around and collapsed in a heap.

Two hours later, the boys at the forensics lab figured out why: strychnine. There was enough in that *cannolo* to kill the whole city council. Later, while fielding one phone call after another (everyone had heard, everyone: ministers, domestic and foreign press, colleagues, citizens), the prosecutor Mandati looked up and saw Teresa and Lucio rushing into the office, pale and shocked.

"I was attacked today in class!" Lucio said.

"But why? How?"

"People say that you don't care about catching the murderers. They're saying that you'd even be happy if they were able to kill Pierfiliberto!"

"And what do you think about that?" Mandati asked his son.

"I don't want to talk about it, Papa."

"You never want to talk about anything, apparently."

"What can I say? That guy is an obsession for you! Get over it!"

"Look, this time it's not me that's after him . . ."

"Come on, get real, for once! Dig deep!"

"Go to the devil for once, son!"

That night he found that the house was empty. Mother and son had moved out to stay with an aunt in Rome. He felt a sharp pang of betrayal, abandoned by those who should believe in him.

Still, it was Teresa who really broke the spell that Berazzi-Perdicò had over him. The first and only time that he managed to drag her out to one of his old school friend's parties, he never forgot the look, somewhere between amazement and commiseration, that Teresa gave him. The party guests were strewn around a grand sitting room: beautiful men and women, businessmen, some local politicos, a couple of senior priests. Berazzi-Perdicò was singing, accompanying himself on the guitar—he had a lovely voice. Everyone jostled to get close to him. It was during a seductive version of the hit song "Crazy Idea" that Ottavio saw Teresa giving him that look. It was her way of saying: "What are you doing here? What do you have in common with this lot?"

He took her aside.

"What's wrong? Aren't you having fun?"

"What world are you living in, Ottavio? Don't you get it?"

"Why? We're not doing anything bad, it seems to me . . ."

"Sorry, but where are the wives of these men? Do you realise that you and I are the only couple here? These women are all whores, my dear Mr. Magoo!"

"Teresa, please . . ."

"Whores!" Berazzi-Perdicò threw his arms up in the air. "What a nasty word! They are 'escorts.' And what harm is it if now and then a man wants to have a bit of leisure . . . You be careful, your Teresa seems to be a bit of a prude . . . you're not marrying a feminist, are you?"

"Enough!"

"Oh, Ottavio, these people are useful to me. They are important for my project. I mean to say, they are useful to *us*. Look, this country is defunct—old, backward. Ideas are not enough; we need legs in order to run with our ideas. It's not my fault that these idiots here have the legs. I would much rather avoid them, but its not possible. You can't. These men that give themselves such airs are, for us, simply idiots with legs. Now, us two, the supermen, will keep the legs and throw the idiots in the sea. My friend, this is the moment of supreme choice: to be a superman today, here, now, with me . . . or an idiot for ever!"

And in that precise moment, Mandati chose to be an idiot for ever—and never once regretted it.

Even his unhappiness at being abandoned by Teresa and Lucio after the pigeon incident slowly diminished. They had their reasons. After all, he thought, he had dragged them into a senseless battle against their will. The people loved Berazzi-Perdicò. They chose him as their representative and he had defended them to the hilt. The prosecutor remembered the poor schoolteacher, Vito. Was this not, for better or for worse, the ultimate meaning of democracy? And who was he to fight against democracy? Wouldn't it be more "democratic" to just let it all go?

At midnight, while he was trying to concentrate on that old movie, "In the Name of the Italian People," Bardolfo and Pistola turned up.

"We've got a confession!"

"It came via the Internet."

"They're called the Free Novere Brigade."

"We traced their I.P. address."

"This time we'll nail them. All the informants have been alerted. The secret service is on standby. It might take a little time, but we'll nail them!"

7

WHILE WAITING FOR THE COMPUTER INVESTIGATIONS TO bear fruit, and while the secret service were doing their duty and the informants were informing, Berazzi-Perdicò evaded a third attempt on his life. It happened on the fourth day after the failed poisoning. The mayor had gone to the Bella Novere nature reserve, on the edge of the San Lampediano woods, for the official opening of the hunting season.

The huntsmen, numerous in this region, were a key part of his electoral base. The president of the local club, renowned for having published a scholarly work called *The Origins of Novere's Hunting Dogs*, presented him with a precision rifle, the .30–06 calibre Browning Bar Stalk Synthetic, especially suitable for wild boar. At the exact moment that Berazzi-Perdicò bent down to examine the sights of the rifle, two 7.65 calibre bullets whizzed past his left temple.

Instantly, a manhunt was unleashed. The San Lampediano woods were besieged by an angry herd of men, who thought they could see shadows behind every larch or cedar, down in the creek, amongst the dense foliage, and in the shade of the rooftops of the huts built along the paths leading down to the valley near the town. The forensic unit converged on the scene in less than half an hour, and was confronted with quite a spectacle. The brave huntsmen of Novere had fired off no less than five hundred shots of every calibre, type and format. Every possible trace or clue was trampled into the ground, stomped on by a hundred feet, all giving breathless chase.

One portly fellow, the accountant Parascalchi-Porata, from Villerbosa, was moaning and clutching a bloodied kneecap, cursing unrestrainedly (for a practising Catholic) at a tall man standing nearby, who was fondling a Beretta. This was the rifle champion Finuoli-Finamore, from Salaperta di Mezzo. He had mistaken his long-time hunting partner for the murderer, and acted accordingly.

The only viable clue that emerged was supplied by an old peasant woman, who, while scattering birdseed to feed her geese, was almost run over by an aubergine-coloured Mini. At the wheel, said the old woman, there was a young man with long hair and an unkempt beard. The worthy woman recalled the first few numbers of the number plate: NO36 . . .

The press went wild. The principal suspect, indeed, the only one: the prosecutor Ottavio Mandati. Teresa and Lucio offered to return to Novere, but Mandati politely declined. (Ah, once again, like Cincinattus, the old Roman leader, how he revels in complacent self-pity!) His wife did manage to tell him that their boy had won a scholarship and was off to study at Edinburgh University.

First in the queue of the aggressors, next to the all-too-predictable Tafano Tafàni, was the daily paper *The Pietrasanta Bolt*. An article written by one Marco Sgambazzi called for, in no uncertain terms, the immediate arrest of the prosecutor, revealed as the hidden mastermind of the murder attempts. But what the devil had he ever done to this Sgambazzi?

Then, slowly but surely, from the depths of Mandati's memory came the connection: Sgambazzi from Versilia. Of course! After the third, or the fourth (he couldn't remember anymore) trial of the mayor where he had acted as prosecutor, this Sgambazzi, at the time a reporter at *The Novere Echo*, had found the courage to note, ironically: "Signor Berazzi-Perdicò is the most unlucky man in the world, either because the worst cut-throats choose him as a political and business partner, or just because he is rather naive, and doesn't know how to choose the right associates." Sgambazzi's career came to a grinding halt.

Some time later, the poor fellow wrote Mandati a heartfelt note—he'd ended up selling doughnuts in Versilia. Ottavio replied with a letter of encouragement and enclosed a little money for him. Now Sgambazzi was back in the game, but on the right side this time, and ready to do whatever it took to be pardoned for the impetuousness of youth.

Things went from bad to worse, when, exactly seven days after the latest murder attempt, Bardolfo and Pistola burst into the office of the prosecutor loaded down with photographs, videos and computer printouts.

"The Free Novere Brigade doesn't exist."

"Or rather: it was created by just one person."

"The young man who drove the aubergine Mini."

"The number plate and physical description match."

"As do the clues from the computer—all the data comes back to him."

"It's just one man, Dottor Mandati: the son. Terenzio Berazzi-Perdicò. He's done everything on his own."

"Shall we bring him in?"

8

No, for God's sake, no! This time he would not be bamboozled—neither by feelings nor by duty. What the hell! You have to draw the line somewhere. What did President Pertini say once? If you're dealing with thieves, behave like a thief and a half!

He got the whole dossier together and ordered Bardolfo to call the mayor.

"Tell him I'm coming over and he'd better be there."

Terenzio. This was the second time they'd crossed paths. As Mandati climbed into the car, he was overcome by memories.

Summer 2000. Operation White Snow was endeavouring to stop drug trafficking among the smart set in the provincial capital. It emerged that a couple of boys from the *jeunesse dorée* of Novere were acting as pushers for their peers in the same social circle. There was surveillance. Wiretapping. At a certain point, the name Terenzio Berazzi-Perdicò popped up. It was ascertained that the boy was using and selling heroin. A junkie through and through. His father had no idea. The boy was picked up with twenty grams of the highest quality stuff, just on the margin between personal use and dealing.

Taken to jail, Terenzio went into withdrawal. He broke down in tears in front of Mandati, and proposed an exchange. Waive the charges. Put him in a home, in rehab, wherever he chose, but not in jail. If he did, the boy would slit his wrists. In exchange, he offered revelations about his father: the numbers of his foreign bank accounts; contact details for underworld bosses with whom his father was in business. He said he hated him, this overbearing father who had always treated him like a fool and never shown so much as a crumb of affection towards him.

Bardolfo and Pistola were ecstatic. Their eyes widened in hope as they looked to the prosecutor.

"What a great day this is, boss! Go for the jugular. Let's give him hell, that bastard. If not now, when?"

All hell broke lose: the father was informed of the arrest. The Pierfiliberto that showed up at the station was a beaten man; he was heartbroken, destroyed. But his testimony contrasted with his son's. He spoke of his love, affection and dedication, of his attempts to remove the boy from the influence of bad company, and he said he was ready to do whatever it took to save him. He showed them medical records that spoke of suicide attempts. Terenzio was a fragile boy—and he was a poor, desperate father.

"I'll do anything to save him, even step aside."

Bardolfo and Pistola were gloating. The wolf comes to surrender to the hunter, tied paws and muzzle . . .

"Go for it, prosecutor, do it now. He's taken a hit. For months he's gone on T.V. preaching the end of the era of tolerance, the need to crackdown on anti-social conduct; for months he's organised marches with the worthies of Novere to 'jolt our consciences'. What a blow—the moraliser with the junkie son! Slap him down! Call the free press. Call R.A.I. T.V. Disgrace him—take back Novere and, above all, give it back to us!"

But Mandati dithered. His conscience rebelled. He went back to Terenzio. The boy was trembling, vomiting, had the shakes, and was bashing his head against the wall of his cell. Breaking all the rules, he allowed the boy's father permission to visit him. He waited outside, watching on the security camera. He couldn't tell what the two were saying to each other and he didn't want to know—he wouldn't dare intrude on the sacred privacy of this meeting.

Pierfiliberto came out after ten minutes or so, devastated.

"My offer stands. I'll step down."

In front of him was a broken man. But Mandati knew he couldn't profit from it. In the desperate eyes of Pierfiliberto, he saw himself as a father. If this happened tomorrow to Lucio, wouldn't I too be guilty? Wouldn't I too beg for clemency? And wouldn't I loathe those who could grant it but refused to help, leaving me powerless in my misery?

"I'm not like you," he concluded, in the end. *Nunc et semper Cincinnatus.* I am always Cincinattus.

He ordered a round of coffee.

"Do you know a good rehab unit, Pierfiliberto?"

"Certainly."

"Take your son there."

"When?"

"Right away."

"I ... thank you ... I don't know . . ."

The same night Mandati asked the magistrate to drop Terenzio from the main trafficking enquiry—the case was filed under "charged for personal use" after a few weeks. One year later, the prosecutor got a postcard from Rotterdam. Terenzio was studying

International Maritime Law there. He was clean. He wanted to let him know that he owed him a great deal.

And so it went. Accompanied by scepticism from Teresa ("He's beaten you again—you're too soft for this world, my love . . ."), were the disappointed and embittered looks of Bardolfo and Pistola. And so it went. He never had second thoughts. I am one thing and he is another. We are one thing and they are another. And that is how the world has to work.

And so it went.

"Not today, Pierfiliberto. Today the rules are changed. We're playing by my rules."

The mayor cast a casual glance at the file, listening without moving a muscle to the police report. He shrugged, sighing, "Have you finished, Otta?"

"I'm not interested in your son. He's just a miserable nutter. Take care of him, and maybe he'll be saved. What interests me is you."

"You know something? I knew that."

"You are the scourge of this city, Pierfiliberto. For as long as you are in charge here, there is no future for the people of Novere."

"Future? And you think they give a damn about the future? You think that if they were capable of thinking, let alone thinking of their future, they would choose me? Come on, Ottavio!"

"Enough chat. I came to propose a deal."

"A deal! But wasn't it you who said that magistrates don't negotiate with criminals?"

"I changed my mind, alright?"

"It would be the first time in your life that you showed a little smarts."

"Do you want your son to spend the rest of his life in a hospital for the criminally insane?"

"I'm listening."

"We'll leave Terenzio out of this affair."

"And the bomb? The poison? The shooting?"

"Filed under unsolved crimes."

"What do you want in exchange?"

"Terenzio, your poor son, goes to recover in a clinic for the mentally ill. And you . . ."

"And I . . . ?"

"You resign from all your positions, sell your properties—or rather, make a nice donation to the community, to the Ministry, or any non-profit organisation that you like, and you get out of here."

"You know something, Ottavio?" Berazzi-Perdicò laughed. "You have never understood a bloody thing about anything. It's no accident that you ended up as a public prosecutor. See, the train of your life arrived, one day, and you let it go by. Back then, I would have been willing to do anything for the boy—but that was then. I wasn't so . . . how can I put it? Sure of myself? And you were always too much of an idiot to understand how things really stand. In other words, now it's time for *you* to push off, my dear fellow."

Berazzi-Perdicò clapped his hands with that theatrical and seductive self-assurance that Ottavio knew all too well. A little door opened. In came Terenzio. Perfectly shaven, smiling, elegantly dressed in pale grey.

"Did you hear, my boy?"

"Everything, Papa."

"And you heard?"

Bardolfo and Pistola nodded.

"Good," Pierfiliberto smiled. "And now, the papers."

Bardolfo and Pistola snapped open the locks on his briefcase (that's strange, Mandati thought, I didn't realise he had that with him) and handed him two folders with pink covers.

"Come on, Ottavio—take a look at the great joke I've played on you. It's just like once upon a time when we were at school, remember? Even then you were sure of winning . . ."

From the folders slipped some snapshots. Mandati picked them up with trembling hands. Click. The prosecutor places a bomb under Pierfiliberto's Lexus. Click. The prosecutor inserts poison with a syringe in a *cannolo*. Click. The prosecutor puts on a disguise and a fake beard. Click. The prosecutor climbs into an aubergine-coloured Mini. Click. The prosecutor, armed with a pistol, fires at the mayor.

"So? What do you say?"

Mandati looked around, bewildered. Bardolfo shrugged. "Boss, there's a mortgage to pay, and I . . ."

"'Fess up, you dirty swine!" Pistola said, eyes bloodshot and index finger jabbing at the prosecutor. "You're a loser, Ottavio Mandati. And I don't have the stomach to keep losing! I want to be a winner too, for once! Get it?"

Mandati caught Terenzio's eye. The boy smiled at him and spread his arms wide, "*Talis pater* . . . Like father, like son . . ."

From the depths of Mandati's being came a terrible howl, like a wounded animal. He took the dossier, the real one, and began to wave it around like one possessed.

"No, no! You can't screw me! None of you can screw me! No-one can! In here is the proof! Here is the truth!"

"Fine," Pierfiliberto said, chuckling. "So there are two truths. Yours and ours."

"You don't even know what truth means!"

"Guilty as charged. But who do you think the people will believe? You, who has hated me for a lifetime, and has always lost, or me, who everyone loves, and who always wins?"

Then, as if on a secret signal, the mayor, his son and the policemen began to hum a hip-hop tune.

Abandon all hope, oh yeah,
Abandon, abandon hope, all hope, oh yeah
Ye who enter here
Abandon
Abandon
Abandon every hope . . .

Mandati swayed, reaching out in vain for a prop, something to support him in the darkness that was rising around him. He found nothing.

9

On March 18, Bardolfo and Pistola presented themselves at 9:00 a.m. on the dot. The prosecutor listened to them with a faint smile, still under the influence of the second dream.

The path to the courtroom. The entrance. The little crowd of supporters of Berazzi-Perdicò, the ambush of Tafano Tafani . . . it was as if he found himself in that film where poor Bill Murray is forced to relive the same day over and over again . . . what the hell was that film called again? But there was a difference: the honour guard walking to the front of the anteroom. Leading it was a young captain from the carabiniere in full uniform, giving a rigid military salute with sabre raised.

Oh come on, that's over the top, Mandati thought.

"At ease. A pleasure to meet you, Captain, I'm Mandati, the prosecutor," he said, approaching him with outstretched hand.

But the captain ignored him and turned around in a graceful pivot, sheathed his sword and hurried over to pay homage to Berazzi-Perdicò, who just at that moment appeared with his jumped-up entourage of shyster cronies.

"All very well," the prosecutor muttered to himself, and then added, "but who cares? Thank heaven for the dream, or rather the nightmare. At least I realise how alone I am. Better alone than in bad company."

"What are you doing, speaking in proverbs this morning?"

Pistola had a really dazed air about him. And Mandati, in spite of the exaggerated calm he felt he had to affect, was dangerously close to losing it. The minute this hearing is over, he thought, I'm going straight to a neurologist.

With great panache, Berazzi-Perdicò stepped forward to shake hands, a gesture which was instantly immortalised by countless flashbulbs. Mandati smiled at him. Berazzi-Perdicò bowed. Mandati squared his shoulders. The judge, the same jolly roly-poly colleague from his dream, came into the room. Everyone jumped to their feet and, just as quickly, took their seats again.

"Now," his colleague said, "today we are dealing with—"

"Your Honour, allow me," interrupted Gianmaria Allegro Appella, the chief defence lawyer, who leapt to his feet. "We have a preliminary objection."

Mandati made a great effort not to be shaken by this, but felt a small pinprick . . .

"What are you referring to, exactly?"

"In our opinion the taping of the telephone calls is inadmissible."

Mandati stifled a laugh. He was aiming high, this prince of the courtroom. But he knew full well why: the case depended on the intercepted calls. Neutralise those, and the trial died. Lawyers always tried it on, even many of those sitting in Parliament, those who were powerful and with, so to speak, a certain amount of balls.

Phone taps had always been their *bête noire*. When they were done properly, they revealed a great deal. In some cases, everything. In this case they exposed a dizzying amount of bribes relating to waste disposal across the whole province. Berazzi-Perdicò got the lion's share. On one recording, a Neapolitan entrepreneur confided to his close friend: "You won't believe how much he asked for." Another had to go to every dealership in the northeast to find the right model and colour of Lexus that the mayor liked. The Lexus, Mandati thought with a smile, that in his dream jumped in the air . . . The mayor's greed was legendary even among his accomplices.

Without the phone taps, in other words, there would be no justice, which is why the lawyers hated them. For this reason, Mandati had been very careful to conduct them with total propriety, according to the rules, without leaving any openings to the defence. The key to everything is motivation. He needed to explain why it was necessary for one guy to be tapped, and also why he used one type of recorder rather than another. Subtleties, to be sure, but they made a difference. Mandati felt he had an ironclad case.

"In our opinion, the authorisation was lacking in motivation pursuant to Article 268 of the procedural code . . ." The lawyer, Appella, approached the bench and gave her a sheet of A4. She took it and began to scan it. Mandati closed his eyes. A few seconds—in one of those impromptu decisions you make on the run, so to speak—and the judge would have denied the objection.

"Prosecution, please come forward . . ."

She just wants to go through the motions, Mandati deluded himself, as he approached Appella, planted in front of the bench.

"What is this stuff, Ottavio?"

"It's the authorisation of the phone tapping."

"And did you write this?"

A feeling of foreboding rose in him. He scanned the page. It was a bad photocopy. *Phone tapping is ordered for the following users . . .* A list followed. Not one line of justification. But this wasn't his style.

"I didn't do this," he said, handing it back to his colleague.

"Someone stood in for you, then?"

"No, I was overseeing it myself."

"And yet, Judge," Appello said, "as you can see, there's Prosecutor Mandati's exact signature at the bottom of the page."

"And this document doesn't have a scrap of just cause," the magistrate sighed, with a note of sincere regret in her voice. And then she added, even more regretfully, "This being the case, the phone tappings are totally inadmissible." A trickle of cold sweat dripped down Mandati's back. He didn't write that damned page. It was trumped-up fake. A lousy fake.

"I don't know where the lawyer got this document," he hissed, furious. "And allow me to cast doubt on its authenticity . . ."

"Judge!" Appella said. "I don't agree that . . ."

"Quiet!" Mandati said, under the astonished gaze of his colleague. "I'll give the administrative order to you now."

He went back to his desk. He had to find the original. He remembered he'd put it . . . he flipped open his file, turned to the page he needed, and . . . But it wasn't possible! This was a real nightmare. The original, the one that was always in his possession, safely in his office, in a cabinet to which only he had the key . . . it was the same junk—senseless nonsense.

"So, Mr. Prosecutor?"

He looked around, caught the mocking gaze of Berazzi-Perdicò, and realised that he had lost. Again. And maybe for ever. He realised also what they had done, and he understood but he was never going to be able to prove it. Someone had been corrupted. Someone had nicked the keys to the cabinet and had substituted the original document with this bullshit. But who? Bardolfo and Pistola were conferring with each other, apparently as surprised and dismayed as he was. Who? A secretary? A young colleague? Who? Who had he trusted? Nobody, surely.

"Better to be alone . . ."

"Now's not the time for proverbs! We have to demand an appeal. That son of a bitch can't get away with this."

Bardolfo stared at him, aggressively. His colleague on the bench stared at him, dumbfounded. Appella stared at him, arrogantly. Everyone stared at him.

Suddenly, a smile appeared on his face—no, a huge grin. For all that he tried to quell it, he couldn't keep it in. He surrendered. There was nothing more to do. He rose, as if in a trance, and moved towards the exit. Behind him, they started to shout, to call him back. But in his ears came only the mocking echo of a tune with a hip-hop rhythm. A tune that went:

> Abandon all hope
> Oh yeah
> Abandon
> Abandon

EPILOGUE

"Papa, Papa! Wake up! What's happening?"

"Ottavio, please, wake up! Ottavio!"

A weak rosy glow filtered through the window. Mandati struggled to focus on the figures leaning over him.

"Look, it's 8:00! In half an hour Bardolfo and Pistola will be here. Have you forgotten what day it is?"

Well, well. He became sure, definitively sure, while sipping the coffee that Lucio had prepared for him, that it was all a dream. Even better, a triple dream. It was March 18. And as the headline of the *Novere Echo* said, THE MAYOR PIERFILIBERTO BERAZZI-PERDICÒ IS PREPARING TO FIGHT HIS UMPTEENTH BATTLE WITH THE PROSECUTOR MANDATI.

Dreams are actually instructive. Because not even in dreams can you get away from the law. "To the thieves, you must be a thief and a half" is a fallacy. There are no shortcuts, and lies have short legs. And the diversion of funds, even the smallest infractions, must be paid for.

Lucio had taken the newspaper.

"It says here, 'The defence has a strategic move in store designed to nip this judicial proceeding in the bud.'"

"Let them say so. It's their job."

"All the same, it seems strange."

"I love you very much. Really, you have no idea how much!"

"Papa, promise me one thing."

"Go on, son?"

"You're trying hard to stitch up that good-for-nothing. But let's say you can't . . ."

"This time he won't get away, Lucio. Believe me."

"But let's say something happens at the last minute . . ."

"Like in the dream."

"Stop carrying on about your dreams!"

"Sorry, go on."

"Promise me this will be the last time. If you lose, accept that he is stronger. Ask for a transfer. We'll all go to Rome, and make a fresh start."

"I promise."

For the first time in years, Lucio allowed his father to embrace him. Ottavio had forgotten the wonderful sensation of physical contact with his child, which made him tremble with delight and emotion.

"This is not an empty promise, my boy. But wait till you see the finale, eh?"

Before he caught up with Bardolfo and Pistola, who were waiting, champing at the bit in their crumpled high-street suits, he went into his office and pulled down a bad reproduction of Hopper's "Nighthawks," revealing the little safe with the combination that only he knew. He rifled through, looking for a transparent plastic file that held the ten pages of his applications for phone tapping. He had decided to keep these to himself as soon as he grasped the devastating power they held for the enquiry.

Berazzi-Perdicò and his cronies would have had to ransack his office, corrupt half the world, fabricate the most sophisticated procedural ploys, construct the most shameless falsification . . .

They hadn't found the file.

Translated by Eileen Horne

ANDREA CAMILLERI, creator of the celebrated Inspector Montal-
bano, is one of Italy's best-loved and most successful authors.
The Potter's Field was the winner of the 2012 C.W.A. International Dagger.

CARLO LUCARELLI was co-founder of the "Gruppo 13" writers'
collective. He was shortlisted for the C.W.A. Gold Dagger in
2003 for the novel *Almost Blue*.

GIANCARLO DE CATALDO is an Italian magistrate turned crime
writer. He is the editor of *Crimini: The Bitter Lemon Book of Italian Crime Fiction*